Robert L. Preston

WAKE-UP AMERICA

IT'S LATER THAN YOU THINK !

Published by

HAWKES PUBLISHING, INC.
156 W. 2170 S. (Box 15711)
Salt Lake City, Utah 84115
In Utah Call: 487-1695
Toll Free: (800) 453-4616

Copyright 1972

by

Robert L. Preston

First Printing, July, 1972
Second Printing, December, 1972
Third Printing, April, 1973
Fourth Printing, July, 1973
Fifth Printing, October, 1973
Sixth Printing, February, 1974
Seventh Printing, October 1975

Publisher & Bookstore Distributer

ACKNOWLEDGEMENTS

The author is grateful to Linda Adams for the valuable assistance she gave with the manuscript, and to John D. Hawkes who is the kind of publisher every author hopes to work with. A special thanks to those who have given so much, that this work might be produced -- my wife and family.

The Author

Dedicated to those who have given me the greatest appreciation of our constitutional freedoms -- my wife, and our precious children.

TABLE OF CONTENTS

Wake-Up America	9
How Has it Happened?	21
The Conspiracy Behind the Conspiracy	27
Capitalism Financing Communism	49
Capitalism Engineers World Take-Over	67
We Won't Have to Attack	81
Knowledge is Not Enough	109

CHAPTER 1

WAKE-UP

AMERICA

WITHIN 10 YEARS YOU WILL BE LIVING UNDER COMMUNIST RULE!

YOU WILL HAVE BARELY ENOUGH TO WEAR AND TO EAT. YOU WILL LIVE WITH STRANGERS AND YOU WILL NOT HAVE A CAR. YOU WILL HAVE A WORK PERMIT. SPEAK YOUR MIND, WORSHIP GOD, OR VIOLATE ANY OF THE RULES OF THE STATE, AND THEY WILL REVOKE YOUR WORK PERMIT. WITHOUT IT YOU WILL NOT BE ABLE TO OBTAIN FOOD, CLOTHES OR SHELTER. YOU WILL BE ARRESTED AS A VAGRANT AND SENT TO A LABOR CAMP. CHILDREN WILL NOT LIVE WITH THEIR PARENTS. THEY WILL LIVE IN GROUPS AND BE INDOCTRINATED TO SERVE THE STATE WITHOUT QUESTION. ALL MEMBERS OF PATRIOTIC ORGANIZATIONS WILL BE ROUNDED UP; THE LEADERS WILL BE INTERROGATED, TORTURED, AND EVENTUALLY SHOT. THE GENERAL MEMBERSHIP WILL BE PLACED IN DETENTION CAMPS AND WORKED TO DEATH. FREEDOM WILL HAVE PERISHED AND AMERICA WILL HAVE DIED!

INCREDIBLE. IT CAN'T HAPPEN, YOU SAY! BUT IT IS ALREADY HAPPENING. WAKE-UP, AMERICA, IT'S LATER THAN YOU THINK!

Some day in the near future, probably on a Friday, you will learn from the news that the stock market on Wall Street in New York has crashed. The wave of selling became so great that the market was closed at one o'clock instead of three. The market fell in that short period nearly 300 points. You will read that what experts had been saying would never happen again has happened, only worse than ever. As people all over America listen for the latest developments over the weekend, they will learn that entire fortunes have been lost, wiped out; millionaires are broke. They will learn that whole companies will be bankrupt and forced to close.

Within two weeks from that bleak day the market will have dropped another 300 points. The President will have ordered the market closed and will have closed the banks. Millions and millions of people will be out of work, probably including you! Prices will plummet; everything will be cheap because everyone will be trying to sell to get a little cash.

Then the cities will begin to see riots, as mobs storm the supermarkets for food they must have but have no money to buy it with. Soon the rioting will spread from city to city. Suddenly every major city in the nation will be engulfed with mass rioting, rioting which began over the necessities of life. Now it will have erupted into a civil war of hate, with a feeling of "this is it!" among minority hate groups that have been waiting for the right moment to strike. Cities will become infernos of fire as bombs explode, gas mains erupt and arsonists sweep through neighborhood after neighborhood. Soon water will be out, the supply will be cut off, the fires will burn uncontrolled. Snipers, hidden from view, will hunt their innocent victims with high-powered rifles; revolutionaries will confiscate food and wealth wherever they find it. Hundreds of thousands will be murdered. Women will be raped and assaulted. Hundreds of thousands more will die of disease and starvation.

The cities will become uninhabitable. Everyone will try to flee from the cities, but there will not be enough gas. Stalled cars will clog the roads and streets and highways. People w.'l be forced to travel on foot. They will take with them only what necessities they can carry. As soon as they venture outside, they become easy prey for the sniper, the gangs and self-appointed destroyers of society.

Governors and the President will declare martial law. People suspected of violating the law will be shot on the spot. But the numbers of riots and fires and cities involved will be too great for the military and the police to handle. Thousands will defect from their military and police posts to protect their own families. America will be in flames, America will be dying!

Eventually the military will suppress the insurrections, and a form of peace will return to the twisted and charred remains of what was once a proud and mighty nation. Special commissions and panels and boards will be convened to re-establish trade and farming and industry. Gradually life and vitality will flow back into the nation. But it will take years. Meanwhile there will be rationing of food. Jobs will be allocated to those who can prove the greatest need, or ability to perform them. Everywhere there will be restrictions and controls and regulations. You will need a permit to travel, to work, and to buy or sell. Your freedoms will be gone, but you will be grateful just to be alive. At first you will not realize that you are a slave of the State. It will all come about so naturally you will think all of this has been done by the government out of necessity.

Gradually through the news media that will be re-established you will be told that all of this came about because the government did not have enough controls on the economy of the nation. You will be told that the experts have studied the matter and feel that it was brought about largely because the Constitution and the form of government that it created was outdated. Times had changed. Things were much more complex and moved much faster than in the days when the Constitution and the government had been conceived. They failed to meet the fast-moving needs of a modern nation, and thus the great calamity befell the country. You will be told that the experts have worked long and hard and have come up with a new constitution that will allow the government to have the controls and regulations of society and life that are needed to prevent such a condition from recurring. You will be told that without the new constitution and government the nation may never recover, that you and your family will be destined to live out the rest of your lives in poverty and disease and destitution. You will be told that unless we quickly adopt this new constitution other nations may be able to descend upon us in this weakened state and overcome us. But if we will go to the polls and in a special election adopt this new constitution, a speedy recovery is assured and we will be safe and returned to prosperity, comfort and convenience.

Willingly, eagerly, like so many sheep, the American people will rush to the polls to adopt a new constitution-- a disguised Communist constitution. In a short period of time you will realize that you are a slave of the State, just one of billions throughout the worldwide empire of Communism.

Seems incredible, doesn't it? Sounds like an apocalyptic nightmare in reverse. Today there are millions upon millions who once thought the same thing, and now they live under the iron boot of Communism. Just a short 60 years ago Communism was only a wild vision in the minds of a few revolutionaries. Just a short 60 years ago. It was then that a small beady-eyed man by the name of Vladimir Lenin announced to the world what at that time must have seemed to have been the most ridiculous of plans for conquering the world. Lenin stated:

> After Russia we will take Eastern Europe, then the masses of Asia, then we will encircle the United States which will be the last bastion of capitalism. We will not have to attack. It will fall like an overripe fruit into our hands.[1]

A LOOK AT THE RECORD

As we look back over the events of the past 60 years, it seems impossible, but they have done everything they said they were going to do and in the exact same manner and order in which they told us they would do it. By 1920 the Communists had taken over all of the area now known as Russia. Then just as outlined they began working on Eastern Europe, and one by one like so many tenpins they fell--Czechoslovakia, Poland, Hungary, East Germany, Romania, Yugoslavia, Albania. Then they began on the masses of Asia, just as they said they would--China, Mongolia, Tibet, Algeria, North Korea, North Viet Nam. Then began the encircling of the United States with Cuba just 90 miles off our shores, then Chili in South America, now Communist guerrillas conducting hushed-up warfare in Mexico and every nation in Central and South America.

As incredible as it seems, Lenin's plan for world revolution has proceeded exactly as outlined. The record tells us that in addition most of Western Europe, Africa and South America is made up of Socialist forms of government that are within a hair's breadth of being openly Communistic. No person can look at the call and plan for world revolution and then look at the record and not know that just as Lenin predicted, the United States IS the last bastion, the last hope of free men everywhere.

KHRUSHCHEV'S BOAST

When Nikita Khrushchev visited the United States, he boasted that the Communists would bury us and that our grandchildren would live under Communist rule. He even outlined the exact manner in which they would accomplish it:

> You Americans are so gullible. No, you won't accept Communism outright, but we'll keep feeding you small doses of Socialism until you'll finally wake up and find you already have Communism. We won't have to fight you. We'll so weaken your economy until you'll fall like overripe fruit into our hands. [2]

As outlined by Khrushchev and Lenin, there is no intention for the Communists to attack us in battle; they expect us to fall into their hands like overripe fruit. They intend to bring this about by weakening our economic structure until we are financially insolvent and by giving us more and more Socialism until we are too weak to resist the final thrust into complete Communist rule. As we review the Socialistic and economic picture in this nation today, we are forced to admit that they have once again proceeded exactly as planned.

SOCIALISM IN AMERICA

Perhaps no greater measure can be made of the effectiveness of the Communist Conspiracy to Socialize us until we fall into their hands than this statement by the six-time Presidential candidate of the Socialist Party, Norman Thomas: " . . . here in America more measures once praised or denounced as Socialist have been adopted than once I should have thought possible short of a Socialist victory at the polls."[3]

The difference between Democrats and Republicans is: Democrats have accepted some ideas of Socialism cheerfully, while Republicans have accepted them reluctantly.[4]

Today the most basic and fundamental freedoms for which our forefathers so valiantly fought and died are gone. The right to own and control property as its owner sees fit has been confiscated in a wave of Socialist legislation. Zoning and planning commissions tell the land-and-property holder what and how he can build and use his property. Wage and price control boards tell the businessman what he shall buy and sell for and exactly how much his profit shall be. Those who insist on making more than the government-commissions-approved profit margin are prosecuted as violators of the law and face stiff criminal penalties. Expropriated from the wages and salaries of the workingman is a large part of his income to be redistributed to other men in the society whether or not it is his wish or whether he feels that it is his responsibility to do so. Parents are forced to send their children to schools which teach curriculum that may be directly contrary to their personal beliefs. These are only the briefest of samples of Socialism in America.

Once we realize that Russia is the Union of Soviet "Socialist" Republics, we can comprehend the meaning of Khrushchev's statement, for Socialism and Communism are one and the same. We are already being Communized. When we wake up from our Socialist stupor, we shall realize that we "already have Communism."

THE AMERICAN ECONOMY

The second point in Khrushchev's boast was the weakening of the economy until we are so weak that we, as Americans, are unable to stand on our own two feet. Lenin said:

> The best way to destroy the Capitalist System is to debauch the currency. By a continuing process of inflation, governments can confiscate, secretly and unobserved, an important part of the wealth of their citizens.[5]

Through the process of inflation, which is the printing of paper money and issuance of credit without currency and any tangible assets behind it, the United States now has in circulation credits in excess of $120 billion, plus an excess of $400 billion in indebtedness. With only $10 billion in gold reserves to back up these obligations which total more than $500 billion, it is obvious why the economy is in such serious trouble both at home and abroad. Our reserves are so low that it is no longer possible to redeem our obligations in gold, and we are forced to devalue the purchasing power of the dollar. So little faith is maintained in the value of the dollar at home that the government must artificially establish wages and prices in order to maintain any degree of stability in its purchasing power.

> The presumption of a spurious value for the currency, by the force of law expressed in the regulation of prices, contains in itself, however, the seeds of final economic decay, and soon dries up the sources of ultimate supply.[6]

Thus in the midst of devaluation, price controls and talk of coming rationing, we sit upon the edge of the financial precipice about to fall into the chasm of economic chaos just as Khrushchev predicted. Once the economic crash occurs, the ever-advancing tide of Communism will descend with full force to take advantage of our weakened condition. Suddenly Americans will wake up to find "you already have Communism."

THE COUP DE GRACE

All prepared and waiting for the right moment is a document entitled "Constitution for a United Republics of America."[7] It was written over a six-year period by some of the most educated minds in the nation. It was financed by grants totaling millions of dollars, not the least of which was one from the Ford

Foundation for $15 million. This document, which the author has reviewed thoroughly in another work entitled **The Plot to Replace the Constitution**, will turn America into a Communist-Socialist Dictatorship as in Russia, China, Cuba, and wherever the republics of Communism exist.

Most Americans, not having even heard of such a document, dismiss the possibility of ever seeing such a thing adopted in this free nation as being completely unrealistic. However, those who have worked so fervently in the background all these years have no intention of seeing their work go to naught. While most of us have been watching T.V., they been gaining real support for their "new constitution." It requires 34 states to pass a resolution calling for a Federal Constitutional Convention to adopt a new constitution for this nation. Out of the required 34, they have already been able to get 33 states to pass a resolution calling for such a Federal Constitutional Convention.[8]

Now all that remains is for this nation to fall over the edge of that financial precipice into an economic crisis similar to the one in 1929--only this one will be much worse--and the stage will be set and the final devastating act will go into motion. When the curtain rings down, the hope of all mankind will be lost, freedom will have perished from off the face of the earth and Lenin's plan will be fulfilled--unless we can wake up in time and throw off our apathy and become involved in this the last battle of freedom. With us rides the hope of all men everywhere. We dare not fail!

WAKE-UP, AMERICA, IT'S LATER THAN YOU THINK!

CHAPTER 2
HOW HAS IT HAPPENED ?

HOW HAS IT HAPPENED?

Perhaps the most amazing thing about the worldwide conquest by Communism is that such unsuccessful and unlikely nations and individuals have been able to accomplish so much. They have been so poor and so outnumbered, while we in the free nations have been so rich and have had so many on our side. So many want to be on our side that the Communist nations have to build walls to keep the people in. Yet in spite of its lack of popular support and its failure to produce adequate goods and services for its people, Communism has continued to expand exactly as outlined by Lenin. How has it happened?

THE REAL CONSPIRATORS

We are all aware of the technique used so successfully by duck hunters of placing decoys in the water to fool the ducks into letting down their natural guard and moving into waters they suppose to be safe only to wake up in the camp of their enemy. We are also aware of Brer Rabbit's deceiving Brer Fox into thinking that the Briar Patch was the hare's mortal enemy, only to have Brer Fox wake up too late and discover that the Briar Patch was in reality Brer Rabbit's best friend. We are also aware that the Communists use many different organizations and groups by various names as front groups. These groups are the decoys--the Briar Patches of the Communists.

The greatest trick, however, has been the use of the Communists as a decoy--a Briar Patch to cover up for the true conspirators. It is not hard to think of who these true conspirators are. All we have to do is imagine that the Communists are Brer Rabbit and then ask ourselves whom they call their Briar Patch. Who is it that the Communists condemn the loudest and the longest? Who is it they claim is their most deadly enemy? Who is it they say they hate? Who is it they heap with abuse and vindictives? Why, it is of course the Super-Rich Capitalist.

Could it be that these Super-Rich Capitalists are the Briar Patch of the Communists? Could it be that the Communists are the front group for them? Could it be that the Communists are being secretly financed and supported in their drive to conquer the world by the Super-Rich Capitalists? Could it be that all of this talk of hate and animosity is merely a smoke screen, a decoy to cause us to relax our natural guard and think we are in friendly waters only to wake up to find that we are in the camp of the enemy? Could it be that the true conspirators to rule the world are really the Super-Rich Capitalists and that the Communists are merely working for them? Could It Be?

BIRDS OF A FEATHER

We are all aware of the old saying that "Birds of a feather flock together." We use it as an example when we wish to demonstrate that people who associate together have common motives and goals. Now let us stop to think about the associations of the Communist leaders of the world when they visit America, the land of their hated enemy the Super-Rich Capitalist. Who do the Communists pose with in the newspaper pictures, shaking hands, arms around each other and smiling at

How Has It Happened?

each other like long-lost brothers? Is it the poor, the downtrodden, the meek and lowly? Is it the laborer and the farmer; or is it the industrialist, the business tycoon--the hated Super-Rich Capitalist? Why, it is the Super-Rich Capitalist! Whenever a top Communist dignitary visits America, he never spends his time with the people--the masses he is supposed to love; he spends all of his time wining and dining with the Morgans and the Watsons and the Rockefellers--the Super-Rich Capitalists.

David Rockefeller, President of Chase Manhattan Bank which is one of the most powerful in the world, has visited Russia several times. Toward the end of the regime of Nikita Khrushchev, Rockefeller became quite outspoken about the negligence Mr. Khrushchev had shown in improving the domestic economy of the Russians. Then in October of 1964 Mr. David Rockefeller, the hated Capitalist, took a vacation in Russia, the land of his supposed enemy. Within a few days after Mr. Rockefeller returned to New York, Nikita Khrushchev was summoned to the Kremlin from his vacation at a Black Sea resort and was informed that he had been fired as the top leader in Russia. Shall we simply dismiss this as strange?

When the avowed Communist Charley Chaplin returned to the United States after an absence of 20 years, an absence that was a self-imposed exile because of his hatred of America's resentment of Communists, he returned in a triumphant wave of adulation created by a special group called the Salute to Chaplin Committee. Oddly enough, the man who headed that committee, the man who was the first American to shake Chaplin's hand as the actor descended from the plane and touched American soil, was David Rockefeller, Jr., the hated Capitalist.

No one who thinks for himself can dismiss all of this as merely strange. If he has any intelligence at all, he can put two and two together and then multiply that by the number of contradictions he has observed in the news between the supposed enemies--Communism and Capitalism. To the thinking person it becomes apparent that the Capitalists must be the Communists' Briar Patch. As the next pages unfold, I will outline in brief the development of the Capitalist Conspiracy to rule the world. Suddenly the confusion and contradictions of the movements of leaders of business and government will clear up. Suddenly the news will begin to make sense. Suddenly you will be able to understand how such a group of unsuccessful nations and individuals can march forward in worldwide conquest, on schedule and according to a predetermined plan. **It happens because powerful individuals behind the scenes make it happen.**

CHAPTER 3

THE CONSPIRACY

BEHIND

THE CONSPIRACY

THE CONSPIRACY BEHIND THE CONSPIRACY

History is filled with the adventures and conquests of those who have sought to rule the world. Some have sought to rule all alone like a king on a throne, while others have worked together in groups. We can all recall the famous line from **Julius Caesar** by Shakespeare, "Et tu, Brute?" as Caesar was turned upon by a conspiracy that involved even his closest friend, Brutus. We can recall with horror the conspiracy of Adolf Hitler and his friends to rule the world and the terrible price that was paid by millions. We can also recognize the terrible price paid by millions as the Communist Conspiracy advances across the globe.

However, the history we wish to examine is that of the Conspiracy behind the Conspiracy--the Capitalist Conspiracy. It begins about 200 years ago.

THE NEW WORLD ORDER

In the year 1776, on May 1, we find the beginning of a new organization. It was called the Illuminati. Its purpose, according to its founder Adam Weishaupt, was to establish a "New World Order" by a select group of "illuminated" gentlemen. The order was set up much like the layers of rings we see on a tree trunk, rings within rings. It was Mr. Weishaupt's intention that each layer was to consider itself to be the innermost layer, until certain individuals within that layer had demonstrated that they could be trusted with the knowledge that was contained within the next layer. Then they would be drawn into the next layer. At the heart or center of this system was a handful of no more than a half-dozen master conspirators who controlled the whole thing.

At this time, there was throughout Europe an increasing interest in knowledge and education. As part of this, there was an increase in fellowship; fraternal and religious organizations sprang up left and right. One of the flourishing organizations was the Free Masons. Weishaupt, who lived in Bavaria where the Masonic Order was very active, saw this as a perfect source from whence to draw his recruits. It is important to realize that although the Illuminati affixed itself to Free Masonry it was a spurious growth, never a real part of the Masonic Order. It was the intention of Weishaupt and his Illuminati to draw into their ranks the richest men of their time. As is so often the case, history now shows us that the rich soon used the Illuminati for their own purposes rather than the other way around.

THE SUPER-RICH

At the time Weishaupt was developing the Illuminati, a very shrewd Capitalist in Frankfurt, Germany, was developing and perfecting a technique for gaining unbelievable wealth and power. He was in the business of loaning money to kings and governments. Of course when one loans money to a king, he may have difficulty collecting if the king decides not to pay back his loan. So Mayer Ahmschel Rothschild perfected a system whereby as terms of the loan he was granted control over all of the nation's currency and credit. Then he very shrewdly gained control over the banking systems of most of Europe by training his five sons in the business and sending them throughout Europe and England to gain control of the various nations' banking enterprises.

Once this was accomplished, all the Rothschilds had to do was made a few requests of the man in power; if he failed to comply, if he refused to pay his debts, they simply removed all of the gold from the bank in his nation to one of their other banks in a neighboring nation and raised the interest rates. This technique caused the economy of the nation to shrink and strangle as the high rate of interest made it impossible for the merchants to expand their trade. This of course was a serious matter for the man in power. As the economy of the nation ground to a halt and the citizens began to be faced with widespread unemployment, poverty and starvation, the ruler became most unpopular and his seat of power was threatened by an uprising of the citizens of the nation. If he foreclosed on the banks in an attempt to take them over and lower the interest rates and stimulate the economy, he would discover that all of the gold was gone. The other nations would not honor his bank notes, and his nation would be economically isolated in a state of abject poverty, easy prey for a neighboring monarch. Thus the crowned heads of Europe and England became acquainted with the economic facts of life. Said Mr. Rothschild: "Give me control over a nation's currency and I care not who makes its laws."[1]

In 1924 Reginald McKenna, who had been Chancellor of the Exchanger of the Bank of England, had this to say about the power of such banks:

> I am afraid the ordinary citizen will not like to be told that the banks can, and do, create money.... And they who control the credit of the nation direct the policy of governments and hold in the hollow of their hands the destiny of the people.[2]

Thus we see that the banks emerged as the unseen powers behind the governments of Europe and England.

CONSOLIDATION OF SECRET POWER

As Weishaupt and his organization sought the power and influence of the wealthy, it is not surprising they soon came into contact with the Rothschilds. To these wealthy bankers who sought to control the wealth of the world, this secret organization was made to order; for through it they could enlist the efforts of men on all levels working to establish a "New World Order," not realizing that this Order would be owned and controlled by the Super-Rich. Through this unique combination, the Illuminati soon spread throughout all of Europe.

Then in July, 1785, a strange thing happened. A courier carrying secret messages to a group in Silesia, now chiefly in northern Czechoslovakia and southwest Poland, was struck and killed by a bolt of lightning. When the authorities of Bavaria examined the secret documents he was carrying, they became very alarmed and the Elector of Bavaria issued an order in 1786, the following year, for the complete suppression of the Order.

Though there were ample grounds to try Dr. Weishaupt for treason and have him executed, for some strange reason the only penalty imposed upon him was expulsion from the country. He chose to reside in exile in Switzerland, a nation which has since become famous as a haven for revolutionaries in exile. Weishaupt was even offered a pension of 80 florins a month. Interestingly enough, this poor professor refused this offer of funds. It causes us to wonder how he was going to live in exile without an income when he was simply a professor without any fortune to rely upon. The only logical explanation is that the Super-Rich who had joined with him used their influence to spare the life of this very valuable ally and provided him with all of the financial support he would need to carry on his work in exile.

THE SUPER-SECRET ILLUMINATI

Weishaupt had anticipated the likelihood of the Order's being discovered and had written to his chief aid: "I have considered everything, and so prepared it, that if the Order should this day go to ruin, I shall in a year re-establish it more brilliant than ever." [3]

While many investigators of Secret Societies dismiss the Illuminati as a potent force in the world after its suppression in 1786, we must conclude after examining the many reliable statements made subsequent to that time that these investigators have either failed to do their homework well or have deliberately tried to cover up the truth.

In the year 1789, the Marquis de Luchet, a leader in the French Revolution, published a paper in an attempt to warn his countrymen that the revolution they sought was being taken over by the Illuminati.

> ...passions interested in supporting the systems of the Illumines...will never relinquish the authority they have acquired nor the treasure at their disposal.... Deluded people...learn that there exists a conspiracy in favour of despotism.... This sociey aims at governing the

world.... Its object is universal domination [through] a series of calamities of which the end is lost in the darkness of time...a subterranean fire smouldering eternally and breaking forth periodically in violent and devastating explosions.[4]

It is as though Luchet were making a prophecy so accurate was his description of the events that have transpired in the next 180 years.

M. Benjamin Fabre points out in his work on Free Masonry, a work the authenticity of which has been established, that as late as 1808 and 1809 a written communication requesting information on behalf of Weishaupt was delivered by the Italian delegate to a Masonic conference in Paris. "And one is led to ask what could be the extraordinary importance of the role played at this moment in Freemasonry of the First Empire by this Weishaupt, who was supposed to have been outside the Masonic movement since Illuminism was brought to trial in 1786."[5]

The author has in his files literally dozens of authentic statements on the continuation and activities of the Illuminati which are being compiled into a complete and comprehensive volume on the work of this secret order. However, the two previous statements will serve our purpose to demonstrate that the Illuminati continued to be active in the affairs of Europe after its supposed suppression in 1786. Not only was the Illuminati active in Europe, but it had also spread to the United States.

THE ILLUMINATI IN AMERICA

Due to the close association with the French during the Revolutionary Period of the two nations and the involvement of the early American patriots in Free Masonry, it was only natural that some of them would become involved with the Illuminati. On the outer levels of the Order, it appeared to pave the way to a better type of life for all mankind. It was only after an individual had worked into the inner workings of the Order that he discovered its true motives. Hence men like Benjamin Franklin, John Adams, Alexander Hamilton and Thomas Jefferson became associated with the introduction of the Illuminati in America. They were even instrumental in having the seal of the Illuminati adopted as the reverse side of the Great Seal of the United States. This took place on June 10, 1782, and it was retained by an act of Congress on Sept. 15, 1789, simultaneous with the adoption of the Constitution.

This seal is found on the reverse side of the one dollar bill. Across the top are the Latin words "Annuit Coeptis," meaning "our enterprise," and across the bottom are the Latin words "Novus Ordo Seclorum," meaning "new world order." This is the motto of the Illuminati. Across the base of the pyramid are the Roman numerals which stand for the year 1776, the year the Illuminati was founded. The pyramid is composed of layer upon layer, each ascending higher and higher and at the same time becoming smaller and smaller just as is the order of the organization of the Illuminati. At the very top is the all-seeing eye which looks out upon all things and oversees the great pyramid.

It is interesting to note that this was not a Masonic symbol until it was adopted at the Congress of Wilheimsbad in 1782, the same year it was adopted as the reverse seal of the United States. This seal has never been cut and used as an official seal of the nation. However, in 1934 Henry Morgenthau, the Secretary of the Treasury, had the seal added to the one dollar bill at the request of Henry Wallace, the Vice-President to President Roosevelt. [6]

As word reached America of the terrible atrocities committed upon the people of France under the direction of the Illuminati during the French Revolution, a wave of rejection swept through the nation. On May 9, 1798, we find the Reverend Jedediah Morse preaching a sermon on the subject at Charlestown. "The Jacobins are nothing more nor less than the open manifestations of the hidden system of the Illuminati. The Order has its branches established and its emissaries at work in America." [7]

Also in that year Timothy Dwight, president of Yale, spoke out against the evils of the French Revolution and the spread of Illuminism in America and asked, "Shall our sons become the disciples of Voltaire and the dragoons of Marat, our daughters the concubines of the Illuminati?" [8]

Also in 1798 we find a letter written by George Washington to a Reverend G.W. Snyder concerning the Illuminati in America. Among other things he stated:

> It is not my intention to doubt that the doctrine of the Illuminati and the principles of Jacobinism had not spread to the United States. On the contrary, no one is more satisfied of this fact than I am. [9]

HAMILTON VERSUS JEFFERSON

Alexander Hamilton became deeply involved in the banking business and was Secretary of the Treasury

The Conspiracy Behind the Conspiracy

under George Washington. Hamilton, a member of the Illuminati, was associated in banking with the Rothschilds of England and Europe. Through their influence, he succeeded in establishing the United States Bank which controlled the credit and currency of the infant nation. Hamilton thought that the backing of these great financial powers would assure the young nation of all the credit and money the nation would need to grow and expand. However, the bankers refused to give full recognition to the value of the Colonial script and eventually raised the interest rates, strangling the economy of the nation. In addition to this, Hamilton worked for the creation of an all-powerful central government which would control everything. It is easy to see the influence these wealthy European Illuminists had on his thinking.

However, with the exposure of the Illuminati's deeds in France and the economic strangulation policies of the United States Bank which was controlled by the European bankers, Thomas Jefferson saw through their manipulations. He became a strong believer in the principle of states' rights and an enemy to big government, which could so easily fall into the control of wealthy and powerful men working behind the scenes. Jefferson became involved in bitter debates with Hamilton, and the two men became political enemies. Jefferson's greatest concern was the rising power of the bankers, and his greatest hope was to have the charter of the United States Bank retired. To demonstrate his feelings about the banks in clear and unmistakable terms, Jefferson said:

> I believe that banking institutions are more dangerous to our liberties than standing armies. Already they have raised up a money aristocracy that has set government at defiance.

The issuing power should be taken from the banks and restored to the people to whom it properly belongs.

If the American people ever allow private banks to control the issue of currency, first by inflation, then by deflation, the banks and corporations that will grow up around them will deprive the people of all the property until their children will wake up homeless on the continent their fathers conquered.[10]

Because of such remarks by Jefferson, England, prompted by the Rothschilds who were by this time in control of the Bank of England, began a series of harassments of American seamen that led to the War of 1812. However, when the charter of the United States Bank was renewed, a treaty was quickly achieved and peace was restored.

ANDREW JACKSON AND THE BANK

Andrew Jackson had been a very tough general for the young country and had earned the nickname "Old Hickory" because like a hickory rod he was tough and willowy and could not be broken. After he became President, he came to know the great power of the bankers in the affairs of government; and his fierce determination shows in these words: "You are a den of thieves--vipers. I intend to rout you out, and, by the eternal God, I will rout you out!" And rout them out he did. Upon re-election in 1832 he did not renew the charter of the United States Bank. As a reprisal, the banks raised the interest rates and attempted to blame

The Conspiracy Behind the Conspiracy

it on Jackson. However, he stood his ground and pointed out to the people that it was the banks that were controlling the currency and the credit, not the President. It worked: the people began to put so much pressure on the banks that they capitulated and dropped the interest rates.

LINCOLN AND THE BANKERS

The International Bankers continued to work to regain control over the economy of the nation. They succeeded in gaining the interests of Salmon P. Chase, Secretary of the Treasury under Lincoln. Chase worked diligently for the passage of the National Banking Act, which had the effect of forcing the government to borrow funds by issuing bonds to the bankers. Later Chase came to realize that he had made a terrible mistake and stated:

> My agency in promoting the passage of the National Banking Act was the greatest financial mistake of my life. It has built up a monopoly which affects every interest in the country. It should be repealed but before that can be accomplished, the people will be arrayed on one side and the banks on the other, in a contest such as we have never seen before in this country.[11]

Because Lincoln had refused to borrow the needed funds with which to finance the Civil War and had instead printed government notes rather than borrowing bank notes, he saved the taxpayers billions of dollars. These notes, which came to be known as the Lincoln

Greenbacks because they were printed in green ink, totaled about $346 million and are still in use by the government today. According to a statement by Wright Patman, chairman of the House Banking Committee, the Federal Reserve reported to him that these notes had saved the taxpayers nearly $50 billion in interest payments. The National Banking Act was passed to thwart Lincoln and force him to obtain his financing from the bankers. At the passage of this act, President Lincoln said:

> I see in the near future a crisis approaching that unnerves me and causes me to tremble for the safety of my country; corporations have been enthroned, an era of corruption in High Places will follow, and the Money Power of the Country will endeavor to prolong its reign by working upon the prejudices of the People, until the wealth is aggregated in a few hands, and the Republic destroyed.[12]

Obviously such a brilliant mind as that of Lincoln was going to prove to be too much for the bankers, and their only hope was to remove him from the scene. In a short time a radical actor by the name of John Wilkes Booth assassinated President Abraham Lincoln, one of the greatest men that ever lived on this earth. Later, as investigators were going through the effects of Booth, they found a secret coded message in his trunk. Many years after this it was discovered that Judah P. Benjamin, the Rothschilds' agent in the South during the Civil War, held the key to the secret message. Thus it came out that Booth was in conspiracy with the International Bankers to do away with President Lincoln.[13]

EUROPEAN BANKERS AND SECRET SOCIETIES

At the same time these events were taking place in America, the whole of Europe was becoming embroiled in a revolutionary spirit. One of the leading Frenchmen of the day was Gougenot des Mousseaux, who in 1869 published a book in which he revealed that a leading statesman from one of the Germanic nations had written him a letter which contained the following information:

> Since the revolutionary recrudescence of 1845, I have had relations with a Jew who, from vanity, betrayed the secret of secret societies with which he had been associated, and who warned me eight or ten days beforehand of all the revolutions which were about to break out at any point of Europe. I owe to him the unshakable conviction that all these movements of "oppressed people," etc., etc., are devised by half-a-dozen individuals, who give their orders to the secret societies of all Europe . . . . The Jewish bankers will soon be, through their prodigious fortunes, our lords and masters.[14]

Thus we see that the bankers were in control of the Secret Societies of Europe and were using them to bring about a series of revolutions which would eventually leave them in complete and total control, heading up the "New World Order" that Weishaupt had sought to set up.

Inasmuch as the previously cited reference mentions Jewish bankers, it is important at this point to touch upon a very sensitive area--that is, the extent to which the Jews are involved in this Conspiracy. My personal feeling, after spending much time investigating the Conspiracy, is that expressed by Chevalier de Malet more than a hundred years ago:

> The authors of the Revolution are not more French than German, Italian, English, etc. They form a particular nation which took birth and has grown in the darkness, in the midst of all civilized nations, with the object of subjecting them to its domination.[15]

I believe that the effort to single out the Jews has been a deliberate ruse used by the Secret Societies to confuse the public and to throw off investigators. I believe that much spurious evidence has been deliberately planted to make it appear to be a Jewish conspiracy while in reality it is a conspiracy of Internationalists, power-hungry men from all nations, a breed unto themselves.

Whatever their nationality and background, it is clear that the bankers were directly involved in the behind-the-scenes manipulations of the Secret Societies and that probably not more than a half a dozen were the masterminds of the whole scheme.

COMMUNISM AND THE WORKINGMAN

As a movement of the laboring class of people began to get underway in Europe and England to improve working conditions and to provide greater stability and security for the trades, they began to assemble in various workingmen's groups. Representatives of workingmen gathered from throughout the Continent and called their meeting an

The Conspiracy Behind the Conspiracy

Internationale to represent its international composition. They were sincere and humble men and began their conference by stating, "Faith in God should be adopted by the Congress. . . . Every vinedresser must have a Bible and not neglect divine service."[16]

However, descending upon these workingmen were members of the Secret Societies who sought to turn these men to their own advantage. One of those who took command was a Frenchman by the name of Lafargue, who shouted toward the end of the Congress, "War on God! Hatred towards God! That is progress! We must shatter Heaven like a vault of paper!"[17]

Others who became actively involved in the workingmen's Internationale were the French Socialist Malon, the Russian Anarchist Bakunin, the wealthy German Socialist Engels, the French Socialist Proudhon and the International Communist Karl Marx. Soon the real workingmen were complaining that with all of the outsiders descending upon the Internationale it could not really represent the workingmen: if it "were to be composed in greater part by economists, journalists, lawyers, and employers, the thing would be ridiculous and would annihilate the Association."[18]

The workingmen sought to preserve their movement for themselves. Two of the more articulate men, both engravers of brass from Paris, sought to prevent the take-over by Marx; they were Tolain and Fribourg. Because Marx had placed in the "Preamble of the Provisional Rules of the Internationale" this statement--"the emancipation of the working-class must be brought about by the working-class themselves"--they sought to have Marx expelled from leadership, "invoking the principle that only working men can represent working men." However, by a vote of 25 to 20 Marx was retained.[19]

In writing to Engels about his success, Marx said:

> I shall go personally to the next Congress at Brussels so as to give the coup de grace to those asses of Proudhoniens...in spite of their efforts the Parisian chatterboxes have not been able to prevent our re-election--I shall give them the stick.... Things are advancing, and at the first revolution, which is perhaps nearer than it seems, we that is to say you and I will have this powerful instrument in our hands.... We can really be well satisfied![20]

As James Guillaume has written about Karl Marx and the Internationale, "Like the cuckoo he came and laid his egg in a nest that was not his own. His plan from the first day was to make the great working-men's organization the instrument of his own views."[21]

Once Marx had gained control of the workingmen's movement, an interesting thing developed, as is recorded by Louis Énault in 1871:

> In March 1865 all the secret associations of Europe and North America were merged in the International Association of Working-men, the Marianne, the Fréres de la République of Lyons and Marseilles, the Fenians of Ireland, the innumerable secret societies of Russia and Poland, the remains of the Carbonari, joined up with the new society. This fusion was made.[22]

Thus the scattered efforts of the Secret Societies were welded into one mighty and powerful group behind the leadership of Karl Marx through the take-over of the workingmen's movement by the "economists, journalists, lawyers, and employers."

COMMUNISM AND THE ILLUMINATI

To comprehend the fact that all of these splinter groups, all of these factions of Socialism and the Secret Societies would suddenly and voluntarily unite themselves behind the leadership of Karl Marx and the Working-men's Association calls for some explanation as to what it was that Marx was doing. First we must recognize that it was not due to his magnetic charm. Almost all historians agree that if Marx was anything, he was obnoxious, arrogant and unpopular. But as Marx had passed through his education, he came in contact with those who had been deeply involved with the teachings of Adam Weishaupt and the Illuminati. Whether it was by accident or by design we may never learn; but there is one incontrovertible fact that becomes very, very apparent to any researcher who has examined the tenets of world conquest as laid down by Adam Weishaupt and then compares them to the Communist Manifesto as created by Karl Marx. Marx created nothing new. The Communist Manifesto is nothing more nor less than the concepts and teachings of Adam Weishaupt and the Illuminati.

As we have already seen, writers of that time stated that the Secret Societies and the bankers were tied together, that from behind the scenes there was but a handful who were calling the plays. We must remember that Marx had gained a strong reputation among the leaders of Socialism of that day for his ability to absorb the concepts of others and then put them down on paper in a new suit. Because of that reputation, a mysterious group about which practically nothing can be learned called the League of Just Men hired Karl Marx to write the Communist Manifesto; and that Manifesto is nothing more nor less than Illuminism in a new suit. From the very beginning of Karl Marx's career he was aided and assisted by the wealthy Capitalists, those who were no doubt secret members of the Illuminati. Thus as Marx played into the hands of the Illuminati, this secret organization, directed by a mastermind group, steered all of the various secret organizations to back the Communist movement which was developing within the workingmen's movement.

The key information tying Communism to the Illuminati has been given to us by the French Socialist Malon. Malon was at first strongly opposed to the obnoxious Karl Marx. Then pressure suddenly exerted upon him by the French police forced him to flee to Switzerland in exile. You will recall that it was in Switzerland that Adam Weishaupt spent his exile. When Malon came back from his stay in Switzerland, he was a changed man. He was now a devoted supporter of Karl Marx and the Communist movement.

On Nov. 5, 1880, Marx wrote to a fellow Communist by the name of Sorg the following words concerning the conversion of Malon and others to Communism: "I need not tell you that the secret strings by which the leaders from Guesde and Malon to Clemenceau have been set in motion must remain between ourselves. We must not speak about them."[23] No doubt the "secret strings" that the Communist leaders dared not speak about were their superiors in the Illuminati. Malon stated that "Communism was handed down in the dark through the secret societies."[24]

The Conspiracy Behind the Conspiracy

Malon, who was a close friend of the Russian Anarchist Bakunin, stated that "Bakunin was a disciple of Weishaupt."[25] Bakunin himself declared in a letter that he wrote to Karl Marx, "You ask whether I continue to be your friend. Yes, more than ever, dear Marx...You see, dear friend, that I am your disciple and I am proud of it."[26] Yes, Bakunin was not only the disciple of Weishaupt but also a disciple of Karl Marx, the leader of Communism--Communism which had been "handed down in the dark through the secret societies" that tied Socialists from every nation together in an international Communist Conspiracy to dominate the world. Warned the French Socialist Jaures, "Beware of the Illuminati, who seek to organize the proletariat on a non-national basis."[27]

It was Bakunin who took the Communist Manifesto to Russia and translated it into the Russian language and was influential in bringing Communism to the attention of a young man who came to be feared in that nation. His name was Lenin.

After the triumph of the Bolsheviks under Lenin, Winston Churchill wrote:

> From the days of Sparticus-Weishaupt to those of Karl Marx, to those of Trotsky, Bela-Kuhn, Rosa Luxembourg and Emma Goldman, this world-wide conspiracy . . . has been steadily growing. This conspiracy played a definitely recognizable role in the tragedy of the French Revolution. It has been the mainspring of every subversive movement during the nineteenth century; and now at last this band of extraordinary personalities from the underworld of the great cities of Europe and America have gripped the Russian people by the hair of their

heads, and have become practically the undisputed masters of that enormous empire.[28]

Thus no less a figure than Winston Churchill, considered to be one of the finest historians the world has produced, has concluded that the revolutionary ferver of Communism is nothing more than the continuation of Weishaupt's Illuminati. Note also that he refers to the triumph of the Communist Revolution in Russia as being the product of individuals from the large cities in Europe and America. We shall now see what he means.

CHAPTER 4

CAPITALISM

FINANCING

COMMUNISM

CAPITALISM FINANCING COMMUNISM

To most of us the statement by Winston Churchill that the triumph of Communism in Russia had its origins in "the great cities of Europe and America" seems a very strange thought. However, as the pages of this chapter unfold, we will trace the documented evidence of the heavy financial involvement of the leading Capitalists from the great cities of Europe and America in the Russian Communist Revolution.

CAPITALISTS FINANCE THE MANIFESTO

As we have already mentioned, Karl Marx was hired to write the Communist Manifesto by a mysterious group which called themselves the League of the Just. They thought so little of Karl Marx that for the next 20 years his name was not even printed on the Manifesto. While little is known about the League of the Just, we do know that it did not lack for funds with which to publish the Manifesto.

According to the research of W.B. Vennard, New York Assemblyman Clinton B. Roosevelt, a wealthy American Socialist, contributed heavily to the financing of the Manifesto. In 1841 Roosevelt published a book entitled **The Science of Government Founded in Natural Law.** In his book Roosevelt detailed setting up a world government almost identical to that propounded by Adam Weishaupt and the Illuminati. He called for the abandoning of the U.S. Constitution as a sinking ship.

Clinton Roosevelt also used his influence on Horace Greeley, another wealthy American Socialist. Both, incidentally, had participated in Communist experiments in America; Greeley was especially active in the one known as Brook Farm. Greeley appointed Karl Marx as a correspondent and political analyst for his paper, the New York Times. In 1848 both Greeley and Roosevelt contributed financially to the Communist League in London to assist in the publication of the Communist Manifesto.[1]

Another of the known financial contributors to the work of Karl Marx was the English millionaire Cowell Stepney, "an enthusiastic Communist and member of the General Council."[2] Of course we are all aware that Frederick Engels was a wealthy German who made heavy financial contributions to Karl Marx.

It is strange indeed that Marx, who was dedicated to the overthrow of the Capitalists, dedicated to the complete destruction of the privileged class of the wealthy, the owners and the administrators of businesses, should be supported by these very same gentlemen. These men that he had supposedly sworn to destroy kept him in bread and wine and with a roof over his head, provided his expense money as he traveled the Continent in the spreading of his evil doctrine, followed him about and lent him their support, and paid for the publication of the Manifesto. It doesn't take too much intelligence, once you have the facts, to see that Communism is not the product of the working class. It is the product of the Super-Rich.

CAPITALISTS FINANCE LENIN

The year is now 1907; the place is London, England; and the man is Lenin, a Russian Communist in exile. He is the leader of a band of 17 dedicated revolutionaries, but he has no money and no place to meet. But a close friend of Lord Alfred Milner, the wealthy Socialist, is induced to come to their aid. This friend is Ramsey MacDonald, Socialist Party leader who later became

Capitalism Financing Communism

Prime Minister of England. MacDonald arranges for Lenin's Bolshevik revolutionaries to use the Brotherhood Church in London's East End as a meeting place for Communist activities. Ironic, isn't it, that the very same Communist revolutionaries that were soon to dethrone God in Russia would get their start in a Christian Church. [3] Of course Lenin and his men are without food and without money; so an American Capitalist who believes in the principles of Socialism gives them a grant of 3,000 English pounds. His name is Joseph Fells, the wealthy soap manufacturer. [4] Is it not strange that Capitalists provided the funds for the publishing of the Manifesto of Communism and that now a Capitalist is financing their revolutionary activities?

Wealthy Lord Alfred Milner had written his friend George Parkin that he, Milner, was becoming more radical and revolutionary. We now learn that he was not jesting. Leon Trotsky has written in his autobiography, **My Life,** that beginning in 1907 he and Lenin were financed by a wealthy English financier. Professor Caroll Quigley states that these loans were arranged by none other than Lord Alfred Milner, founder of the Round Table groups and key member of the Secret Society.

It is at this point in time that Paul Warburg came to the United States from the very successful German financing firm, House of Warburg. The Warburgs were closely tied in with other International Bankers of Europe, especially the Rothschilds. In the United States the Warburg brothers united with the Kuhn, Loeb firm and the Rockefellers through the merger of their banks, while in Europe they were connected with the Rothschilds, who were in turn allied with J.P. Morgan. Morgan was united in England with Edward Grenfell and, through Benjamin Strong, with Montague Norman and the Bank of England. Thus, through the connecting link of the Warburgs all the great banking dynasties were united. While these firms were ostensibly in competition with each other, it was a very cooperative kind of competition.

Beginning in the year 1907, the year Lenin was in London, Paul Warburg at a salary of $500,000 per year paid by the Kuhn, Loeb firm began a six-year campaign to educate the American bankers on the advantages of a Central Banking system. It was during this campaign that Morgan, Rockefeller and the other top leaders of the banking firms met in a secret meeting on Jekyll Island, off the Georgia coast, in 1910. This behind-the-scenes conspiratorial cooperation among the top banking firms resulted in the passage in 1913 of the Federal Reserve Act, which gave the International Bankers control of the finances of the United States.

Meanwhile the Russian Communists were having a difficult time establishing themselves. They were constantly being suppressed by the Tsar of Russia. Lenin, in spite of his financial help from Lord Milner and his wealthy Capitalist friends, failed to win enough support in the 1907-1910 Revolution; and he was forced to flee to Paris. While in exile, Lenin continued daily correspondence with his followers in the Social Democratic Party. The Social Democrats continued the fight for greater democracy in government affairs, and Lenin continued his fight to turn the Social Democrats into pure Marxists. In 1912 Lenin moved his base of operations closer to home, in Cracow, Poland. Two years later the First World War broke out, and Lenin was arrested on trumped-up charges of spying for his enemy the Tsar. After two weeks, Lenin was released to go to Switzerland. Lenin stayed in Switzerland for the next three years. You will recall that this is where Weishaupt spent his exile and where the French

Socialists were mysteriously converted by "secret strings" to Communism. While Lenin stayed in Switzerland, his chief assistant Leon Trotsky was sent to London and New York.

GERMAN CAPITALISTS AID LENIN

In an official Russian publication put out to celebrate the 100th anniversary of Lenin's birth, a publication entitled simply **Lenin**, page 21 states, "With great difficulty and with the support of the Swiss Social Democrats, Lenin finally succeeded in organizing the return home of a group of Bolsheviks and other emigrés via Germany, the only way open to them at the time."

This is a very revealing statement. The Swiss Social Democrats made the arrangements for the return of Lenin to Russia. This return was through Germany. Interestingly enough, they fail to mention how it was that a group of Russian exiles were able to return through Germany, who was at this time at war with the Russians. The truth of the matter is that a sealed train was provided, and Lenin and his "group of Bolsheviks and other emigrés" were secretly transported across Germany into Sweden, from whence they easily slipped across the border into Russia. [5]

The Germans also supplied Lenin with a great deal of money. The Russian refugee Bourtzeff has stated, "I affirm, that since August 1914, and in a relatively short lapse of time, the Germans handed over personally to Lenin more than 70,000,000 marks for the organization of the Bolshevist agitation in the Allied Countries." [6] A high official of the German Social Democratic Party through whom the Swiss Party had made the arrangements for Lenin stated in the official party paper, **Vorwarts**, "that he knew as far back as December 1917 that Lenin was in the pay of Germany.

More recently, Bernstein has learnt from 'a responsible person' that the sum given to Lenin was more than 40,000,000 gold marks." [7] The chief arranger for these financial stipends to Lenin was Max Warburg, the brother to Paul Warburg who had been sent to America by the European Central Bankers to gain control of the money of the United States. [8]

Of course all of this could be interpreted as a clever ploy by the Germans. The Russians could hardly handle a civil war and a war with the Germans at the same time. Thus, when Lenin was sent back to Russia in 1917, the civil turmoil that had already been created was about to topple the reign of the Tsarists. For the Germans had been busy, through the alliance of the Social Democratic parties of the two nations, creating all types of disturbances within the country. Strikes, sabotage and disturbances of all types were being promoted and financed by the Germans. In the **British White Paper on Bolshevism in Russia** we find it stated by an Englishman, a Reverend B.S. Lombard, who had been through the whole of the Revolution that "The Germans initiated disturbances in order to reduce Russia to chaos. They printed masses of paper money to finance their schemes; the notes, of which I possess specimens, can be easily recognized by a special mark." As a result of these efforts the Tsarist regime fell and a Provisional Government was established. [9]

The Provisional Government wanted to consolidate the strength of the nation and to fight the Germans tooth and toenail until Russia had been saved. At first the Provisional Government was successful in holding down and finally driving Lenin from Russia altogether. But by the fall of 1917, Trotsky had returned from New York and had brought with him large sums of money and a gang of cutthroats which he had hired. These mercenaries became Lenin's Shock Troops. [10] With these vicious troops and the additional funds, Lenin stormed the seat of government and succeeded in overthrowing the Kerensky regime of the Provisional Government. For 10 terrible days Lenin and his Shock Troops slaughtered all known and even potential resistance.

BRITISH CAPITALISTS FINANCE COMMUNISM

Then once in power Lenin negotiated a peace agreement with the Germans. The Germans were then able to remove the bulk of their troops from the Eastern Front and shift them to the Western Front to fight the English and Americans. It would then make it seem as if the Germans had been using Lenin to their advantage, but this does not explain the fact that both the English and the American Capitalists contributed vast sums, only to have the Russian Communists settle with Germany, freeing the Germans to kill more American and English boys.

The White Russian, Arsene De Goulevitch fled to France after the Bolshevik Revolution, where he founded the Union of Oppressed Peoples, for refugees from Communism, and wrote a book entitled **Czarism and the Revolution**. In this book he states:

> The main purveyors of funds for the revolution, however, were neither the crackpot Russian millionaires nor the armed bandits of Lenin. The "real" money primarily came from certain British and American circles which for a long time past had lent their support to the Russian revolutionary cause. Thus Trotsky, in his book, My Life, speaks of a large loan granted in 1907 by a financier belonging to the British Liberal Party. This loan was to be repaid at

some future date after the overthrow of the Czarist regime. According to Trotsky, the obligation was scrupulously met by the revolution. The financier just mentioned was by no means alone among the British to support the Russian revolution with large financial donations.[11]

Cleon Skousen identifies this wealthy Englishman as Lord Alfred Milner and says, "By 1917 the major subsidies for the revolution were being arranged by Sir George Buchanan and Lord Alfred Milner (of the Morgan-Rothschilds-Rhodes confederacy)."[12] This would agree with De Goulevitch, for he goes on to say, "In private interviews I have been told that over 21 million roubles were spent by Lord Milner in financing the Russian Revolution."

This is very interesting, especially when related to the fact that a footnote to the preceding information concerns the dairy entry of General Janin for the date of April 7, 1917:

> Long interview with R., who confirmed what I had previously been told by M. After referring to the German hatred of himself and his family, he turned to the subject of the Revolution which, he claimed, was engineered by the English and more precisely, by Sir George Buchanan and Lord Alfred Milner. Petrograd at the time was teeming with English.... He could, he asserted, name the streets and the numbers of the houses in which British agents were quartered. They were reported, during the rising, to have distributed money to the soldiers and incited them to mutiny.[13]

Capitalism Financing Communism

All this is verified by Bruce Lockhart in his book, **British Agent**. He describes how Milner went himself to Russia and spent two weeks there on certain business in January of 1917. This was 10 months preceding the Bolshevik Revolution.[14]

BRITISH AGENTS DIRECTED LENIN AND TROTSKY

Later when Lenin and Trotsky were in power Lockhart was assigned as special agent to Russia, "not by the Foreign Secretary but by the War Cabinet-- actually, by Lord Milner and Mr. Lloyd George."[15] The Bolsheviks were not as yet recognized by the English government; nevertheless when it came time to go to Russia, Lockhart was instructed by Milner to go to a certain Russian there in London by the name of Maxim Letvenoff. Although Lockhart had never met Letvenoff before, nevertheless Letvenoff wrote the following letter of introduction:

Citizen Trotsky, People's Commissary for Foreign Affairs.

Dear Comrade:

The bearer of this, Mr. Lockhart, is going to Russia with an official mission the exact character of which I am not acquainted. I know him personally as a thoroughly honest man who understands our position and sympathizes with us. I should consider his sojourn in Russia useful from the point of view of our own interests.

Maxim Letvenoff[16]

Lockhart would hardly need to say more than present this letter; the contents make it quite clear that Milner's man was going to be a definite asset to the Communists.

This agent on behalf of Milner describes his long meetings with Trotsky and Lenin and also describes sitting in on the council meetings of the ruling hierarchy of the Bolshevik regime; naturally he does not reveal what really took place. But it is very difficult to understand how this British agent, on an unofficial mission from a country with which no diplomatic relations had yet been established could have such free and ready access to the two top leaders of the Soviet, especially in the spring of 1918 when they both had their hands more than full with problems of controlling the vast land they had just gained. How is it that he could have their private telephone numbers, call them any time he wished day or night, and demand and get two-hour conferences? How is it that Mr. Lockhart could have a pass signed by Trotsky which read as follows?

> I request all Organizations, Soviets and Commissars of Railway Stations to give every assistance to the members of the English Mission, Messrs. R.B. Lockhart, V.L. Hicks, and D. Grastin.
>
> L. Trotsky
>
> P.S. Personal stores of provisions not to be confiscated.
>
> L. Trotsky [17]

Lockhart had, as he describes it, the run of the land, coming and going where he wanted, when he wanted. He had specific instructions from Trotsky himself for the Soviets to give him "every assistance," and that his "provisions not...be confiscated." Why would he be introduced to Trotsky as a a man who should be considered "useful from the point of view of our own interests"?

None of this makes sense at all if we consider Lockhart as a representative of the British government; but if we consider Lockhart to be the personal representative of Lord Milner, the financier of Communism and the Secret Society, then it all fits. It was not the British government which gave Lenin and Trotsky millions of dollars in aid; it was Milner and his Secret Society, because he had grown more "radical & revolutionary than I then was & less induced to trust in the growth of Federal union from a small beginning." Therefore when Lenin had come along in 1907, Milner saw this as his chance to revolutionize the world quickly.

Lenin tried several times to bring about revolution in Russia and he failed; it was not Lenin who brought about the Bolshevik Revolution, but the members of the Secret Society, members in Switzerland, Germany, England and America, who contributed and manipulated behind the scenes to bring it about. The plan had been worked out years in advance. When it was discovered that the Russians were too strong to be easily overthrown, a war was instigated to weaken the Tsarist regime at home and to allow the revolutionaries, with much financial help, eventually to get control.

AMERICAN CAPITALISTS SUPPORT COMMUNISM

The American Capitalists were there too. By the time that the Bolshevik Revolution took place in 1917 the Federal Reserve Act of America had been passed and Paul Warburg had been placed on the Board of

Governors. It was to Paul Warburg that Leon Trotsky turned for assistance in raising the capital that was needed to finance the Revolution. Warburg was a partner in the Kuhn, Loeb firm on Wall Street in New York. How much money did Paul Warburg raise among the wealthy American Capitalists to help the Communists establish themselves in Russia? We may get some indication by the fact that "Mr. Bakhmetiev, the late Russian Imperial Ambassador to the United States, tells us that the Bolsheviks, after victory, transferred 600 million roubles in gold between the years 1918 and 1922 to Kuhn, Loeb & Company."[18] It is obvious that Paul Warburg had done a good job for his Communist friends, just as his brother Max had done in Germany.

One of the other partners in the Kuhn, Loeb firm was Jacob Schiff. On Feb. 3, 1949, the **New York Journal-American** reported: "Today it is estimated by Jacob's grandson, John Schiff, that the old man sank about 20,000,000 dollars for the final triumph of Bolshevism in Russia."

It is hard to understand, from the traditional view of national loyalties, why German, American, and English Capitalists would spend so many millions of dollars for the establishment of Communism in Russia, especially when it is realized that these nations were all at war and on different sides. It is difficult unless we are aware of the fact that they were all part of a Secret Society which was seeking to bring about a one-world government. How closely they were all tied together is most revealing. Before coming to America the Schiffs had shared a commercial building with the Rothschilds in Germany; they then sold out to the Rothschilds and bought their partnership in the Kuhn, Loeb firm with the money. The Rothschilds were allied with Morgan in America and Milner in England.[19] From the earliest days of the Secret Society Lord Rothschild had been allied in it with Lord Alfred Milner.

While Max Warburg was the head of the Secret Police of Germany and the head of finance for Germany during World War I, his brother Paul was head of the financial machinery of America, the Federal Reserve Board. When this was discovered by Congress in 1918, Paul was asked to step down, which he did quietly without a word of protest.[20] However, he did not step quietly into the background: he became influential in many of the big corporations of the day, corporations such as Western Union, Westinghouse, Wells Fargo, Union Pacific, Baltimore & Ohio, Afga-Ansco, National Railways of Mexico, International Acceptance Bank and Warburg Company of Amsterdam, just to name a few.[21] When the War was over, he was appointed a member of the committee to go to Versailles to work out the peace treaty. His brother Max was there also, representing Germany.[22] Documentation introduced at the Nuremberg trials proved that Max Warburg had also been involved in the financing of Hitler.[23]

AMERICAN AGENTS DIRECT LENIN AND TROTSKY

Just as Milner protected his investment in the Bolshevik Revolution by sending Lockhart to see that everything went off all right, so the American Capitalists sent Raymond Robins under the pretense of being a Red Cross representative. However, just as with Lockhart, he was able to command audiences with Lenin and Trotsky any time that he wanted to. He was also given freedom to travel throughout Russia at will. He told Lockhart that although he was a wealthy man himself he was an anti-Capitalist. He also said that one of his great idols was Cecil Rhodes, founder of the Secret Society.

One of the incidents that took place between Robins and Lenin demonstrates the power that he had over Lenin and indicates that he was far more than a mere representative of the Red Cross. Lockhart relates:

> I returned from my interview to our flat only to find an urgent message from Robins requesting me to come to see him at once. I found him in a state of great agitation. He had been in conflict with Saalkind, a nephew of Trotsky and then Assistant Commissar for Foreign Affairs. Saalkind had been rude, and the American, who had a promise from Lenin that, whatever happened, a train would always be ready for him at an hour's notice, was determined to exact an apology or to leave the country. When I arrived, he had just finished telephoning to Lenin. He had delivered his ultimatum, and Lenin had promised to give a reply within ten minutes. I waited, while Robins fumed. Then the telephone rang and Robins picked up the receiver. Lenin had capitulated. Saalkind was dismissed from his post.[24]

What possible explanation can be given for such extraordinary power over the dictator of the Soviet Union, power to have a train ready to go where he willed on an hour's notice, power to demand certain actions from this man who professed such strong hatred of Capitalists that he would tolerate taking orders from one of them? What can explain the power of Robins to demand the dismissal of a top Party official, a relative of Trotsky and friend of Lenin, demand it and get it, all of this at a time when officials of other nations were being imprisoned and shot on the slightest of excuses?

There is only one explanation and that is that he, as

Capitalism Financing Communism

with Lockhart who worked closely with him, was in reality not a representative of any nation or any legitimate organization. He was the American representative of the Secret Society, and as such he was the boss.

It goes back to what Rothschild said in the beginning, "Give me control of a nation's currency and I care not who makes its laws." Lenin made the laws, but the International Financiers put up the capital. They controlled the currency, not only in Russia but in all of the major countries of the world, and Lenin knew it. Lenin knew that just as they had engineered him into power, so they could bring him down. He knew that they could arm Germany, or Japan, or Italy and wage a war that would wipe him out. The International Financiers were his boss and he knew it. All of the talk about the Communist hatred of Capitalism is just so much show, designed to fool the people of the world into believing that they are enemies. It is another ruse, another disguise, another deception for the Capitalists.

CAPITALISTS GAIN CONTROL OF RUSSIA

No doubt the real reason Russia was selected for the establishment of Communism was the Tsar would not allow the International Bankers to set up a Central Banking System in Russia. He retained absolute government control over the currency of the nation. One of the key stratagems of the Conspiracy, from the time of Weishaupt on, was to gain control of a nation's currency through a Central Banking System. Marx reiterated this policy in the Manifesto, and the International Bankers followed this practice in an undeviating course. Since the Tsar was too smart to let the Capitalists get their hands into his pocket, he had to go. Because the Communists were anxious to bring about revolution, the Capitalists were only too happy to help out. By financing the Revolution they gained the control of the leaders of the Kremlin.

SUMMARY AND CONCLUSIONS

Beginning with Adam Weishaupt and the Illuminati a plan was created, with an organization to implement it, that would bring the entire world under the control of just a few behind-the-scenes manipulators. The International Bankers and Financiers soon saw the value of this plan and utilized their great wealth to get control of it and use it for their own benefit. They were motivated by the thought that once the world was united and under their control they would be able to use the great power of their reason to solve all of the problems and man would be able to live in peace and plenty. The value of this goal was so great that to them it justified the use of any means to achieve it.

By the beginning of the twentieth century a Secret Society was established which had the support of all the major international banking institutions. This Society, though of a secret nature, was no doubt only the outer edge of the true inner circle of a half-dozen key figures in the international banking world. Uniting together, bankers in divergent nations placed many hundreds of millions of dollars at the disopsal of the leaders of Communism and financed its triumph in Russia. Through this financial aid, a dependence was developed as well as an awareness of the true world power of this master group that forces the Communist leaders of the world to be obedient to it. Thus we see the meaning of Winston Churchill's words that the triumph of Communism in Russia had its origin in "the great cities of Europe and America."

CHAPTER 5

CAPITALISM

ENGINEERS WORLD

TAKE-OVER

CAPITALISM ENGINEERS WORLD TAKE-OVER

We have now seen that Super-Rich bankers gained control of the Central Banks of Europe and England and through them gained a great degree of control in the affairs of government. We have also seen that they gained control of the Illuminati, the central organization of all the Secret Societies, and through that means gained control of the Communist movement and impregnated it with all of the teachings and ideologies of Adam Weishaupt. Then they provided all of the necessary financing for the triumph of Communism in Russia. Through Lenin they announced to the world a plan for world conquest. We have seen that they have followed that plan to the letter with undeviating success. This plan called for the military take-over of most of the world through Communism. In the face of a great giant like the United States, Communism would never have been able to make its fantastic world wide strides except for one thing--just as the conquest of Russia by Communism was made possible by the Capitalists, so has been the Communist conquest of the rest of the world.

HUMANITARIAN CONCERN--MISGUIDED

The study of history reveals that there have always been enormous numbers of people who have been born, lived and died in squalor, sickness and misery. Always there have been two groups of men who have looked upon such conditions in a different light. One group sees in the underprivileged only the opportunity for exploitation for their own gain, and the other sees in them a great need for help and assistance. All too often those who seek to help the downtrodden are themselves exploited in the process by the group which seeks to exploit all mankind for its own ends.

From the days of Plato and no doubt from the days of even more ancient philosophers many men have come to the conclusion that most men cannot manage their own affairs with sufficient dexterity and skill so as to arrive at a decent level of living for themselves and their families. Therefore, these men believe in a strong type of paternal government to look after us simple folks who they believe can't look after ourselves. They want to protect us from ourselves and the exploiters.

One such man was a professor at Oxford University. His name was John Ruskin. Ruskin was a devoted fan of Plato's **Republic**, a book which outlines a form of government that establishes a ruling aristocracy that benevolently rules the masses. As the years passed by, Ruskin moved further and further to the left in his thinking and teaching. He dreamed and taught of a world united together, every nation a single state in a world organization, ruled by wise and benevolent men for the good of the rest of mankind. Ruskin came to identify his own thinking with that of the Communist movement, stating, "Of course I am a Socialist-- of the most stern stuff . . . a Communist of the old school." [1]

PLANTING THE SEED

The students of John Ruskin were the sons of the wealthiest men of Europe, America, and especially England. He taught them his vision of the world united and ruled by an elite class of men--men, he told them, of their calibre. Some of his students caught the vision of what Ruskin was saying and caught it in a big way. One of those was Cecil Rhodes. Rhodes devoted his entire life to the expansion of the British Empire with the

Capitalism Engineers World Take-over

dream that someday it would rule the world. Even in death Rhodes was true to his vision for he left his entire fortune to this purpose.

DUPLICATING WEISHAUPT

We shall no doubt never learn the source for all of the ideas that Cecil Rhodes sought to carry out, but it is interesting to note that as a means of carrying out his vision of world rule he decided to organize a secret society. In writing to William T. Stead, a London newspaper publisher, Rhodes wrote of his dream and that it would take "100 years and a secret society organized like Loyola's." [2] This was the exact plan of Weishaupt! Even more reminiscent of Weishaupt is this statement again to Stead in a letter: "the only feasible thing to carry out the idea: A secret society gradually absorbing the wealth of the world."

Did Rhodes get such ideas from secret meetings with his teacher John Ruskin? Did he get them from his private studies, private associates, or did he get them from a business associate, a man who had made it possible for Rhodes to earn millions and millions of dollars to spend on his Secret Society. We may never know for sure; but when the Secret Society was formally organized on Feb. 5, 1891, one of those named to the inner circle was the International Banker Lord Rothschild, his financier. This Society was organized exactly like the Illuminati, with rings within rings.

MILNER THE REVOLUTIONARY

When Rhodes died, he left his fortune to the care of Lord Alfred Milner. Milner soon set about organizing an outer ring, a semi-secret group known as the Round Table. This organization has continued in activity down to the present time, according to historian Caroll

Quigley. These men began to infiltrate government service under the capable direction of Milner. Their objective was to establish a one-world government with them and their superiors in charge. However, progress was very slow and as Milner began to get on in years he became impatient. He wrote to a friend, George Parkin:

> The experience of life has been to confirm extraordinarily my belief in the doctrines which we both held & preached theoretically, as young men, only I am more radical & revolutionary than I then was....[3]

How radical he became is attested to by the fact referred to in the previous chapter that he gave $20 million of his personal fortune to help finance the Communist Revolution in Russia and directed much of what went on there through his personal agent, Bruce Lockhart. Through the Secret Society and its many rings of outer organizations, Milner and his friends were beginning to place men in important positions both in and out of government. England was moving deeper into Socialism, and the First World War was an excellent tool to convince people that it was time to organize on a worldwide basis.

FAILURE IN PARIS

At the conclusion of World War I the representatives of the various governments met in Paris. A large number of these men were members of some level of the Secret Societies. A big thrust was put on to use that set of circumstances to establish a "New World Order." But the Super-Rich were pushing too soon. They had not gained enough control over the will of the people in the United States. Even though they had gained the support and leadership of the President, it was not enough. The

Capitalism Engineers World Take-over

people and the Senate were not ready to plunge the United States into a world government where we would only be one among many; Americans still loved their independence. Thus, even though the efforts of President Woodrow Wilson and others produced the League of Nations, the forerunner of the United Nations, the League never became a great power because the United States never joined. The "New World Order" dreamed of by the leaders of the Secret Society from the founding of the Illuminati by Weishaupt in 1776 down to the Circle of Initiates and the Round Table of Milner and Rhodes almost came into being.

A NEW BEGINNING

The leaders of the Secret Society were naturally disappointed at the failure of their efforts, but they were not discouraged enough to give up. They learned a very important lesson from this experience--America was the stumbling block. America would have to be broken down and conditioned to accept the idea of world government. Americans would have to be convinced that they could no longer be independent.

It was at this point a new plan was developed by the Capitalist Conspiracy and announced to the world by Lenin. He stated that the First World War had given the Communists Russia and that "the Second One will give us East Europe." He then went on to outline that after that the Communists would take the masses of Asia and then ring the United States. They would not attack the United States; they would so weaken the economy and morality through Socialism that it would lose the strength of its independence and fall like an overripe fruit into the hands of the "New World Order."

AMERICANS AND THE SECRET SOCIETY

On May 19, 1919, a meeting was held at the Majestic Hotel in Paris, France. In attendance were the leaders of Milner's Round Table groups--all wealthy men closely tied to the International Bankers, especially to the Rothschilds-- and wealthy Americans all closely tied to the International Bankers, especially through the firms of Morgan, Rockefeller, Kuhn-Loeb, and of course once again the Rothschilds.

Leader of the American group was "Colonel" Edward Mandell House, the English-educated son of a financier who represented various foreign banking interests in the South. House had majored in political science in school. In 1912 he authored a book entitled **Philip Dru, Administrator**. While it was supposed to be a novel, history shows that it was in reality a blueprint of what House intended to do with his own life as an "administrator" in the affairs of government. This is significant because the hero was working to set up a "one-world government as dreamed of by Karl Marx." Now that we know the nature of "Colonel" House's political philosophy it is easy to comprehend the results of what he did.

As a result of this meeting, it was decided to set up The Institute of International Affairs. This Institute "founded at Paris in 1919 was comprised, at the outset, of two branches, one in the United Kingdom and one in the U.S. . . . " [4]

By 1921 the American branch had its charter all written by "Colonel" House, the man who sought to set up a "one-world government as dreamed of by Karl Marx." The board of directors had been selected. Among them was Paul Warburg, the founder of the Federal Reserve Bank, and the organization was officially incorporated as the Council on Foreign Relations. In just six short years House was able to induce the Rockefeller Foundation and the Carnegie Foundation to support the activities of the Council. In 1929 the Rockefellers presented the Council with their

Capitalism Engineers World Take-over

very stately New York headquarters located directly across the street from the Russian Embassy to the United Nations. Now keep in mind that the Rockefellers donated the land and building to the Council, this organization that was dedicated to establishing the "one-world government that was dreamed of by Karl Marx"; and they also years later donated the land for the building of the **United Nations, which was founded by leading members of this Council on Foreign Relations**, several of which it was discovered later were Communist agents.

THE CFR IN WORLD WAR II

By the time the United States was pulled into the Second World War the President was surrounded by advisors and members of his administration that were members of the Council on Foreign Relations. Winston Churchill kept trying to get Roosevelt and Stalin to agree on a major assault on the German forces from the south up through Italy in what he called the soft underbelly. Had this been done the War would have ended with a different division of lands, a division that did not fit with the plans of the Council for a new world government. Thus Roosevelt's advisors kept insisting on an attack across Europe by the Americans and an attack by the Russians from the east.

This was proposed for three strategic reasons. The first was that the European nations would be so ravished by war that they would be too weak and tired of fighting to resist the organization of a new world government once the War was over. The second was to get the United States to supply Russia with badly needed money, materials, and equipment, not so much to fight the War as to build herself into a major power once the War was over. Third was to give Russia access to the nations of Eastern Europe, thus letting the Second

World War give the Communists Eastern Europe as Lenin had predicted.

It is of interest to note that General Patton, who had a very intense hatred of Communism, kept pushing his men on toward Czechoslovakia in order to beat the Russians; it was his hope that the Americans would be able to liberate the East European nations. To the north the Ninth Army was within hours of taking Berlin. Suddenly both were told to hold up; they were given specific orders to allow the Russians to move into those areas. Who gave that order? It was Dwight D. Eisenhower, a member of the CFR.[5]

At the conferences held at Yalta and Teheran where the deals were made between Roosevelt and Stalin as to how the territory was to be divided up, standing at Roosevelt's side was his top advisor urging him to give up East Europe and Berlin to the Russians. Who was that advisor? It was Alger Hiss, a member of the CFR who was later convicted as a Communist spy.

Did President Roosevelt know that Alger Hiss was a Communist when he took Hiss with him as an advisor to those conferences? Martin Dies, chairman of a Special House Committee on Un-American Activities, has testified before the Congress that he personally took a list of more than a thousand names of men like Hiss who had infiltrated the government as agents for the Communists. Dies stated that Roosevelt became furious at him, saying:

> I have never seen a man who had such exaggerated ideas about this thing. I do not believe in Communism any more than you do but there is nothing wrong with the Communists in this country; several of the best friends I've got are Communists.[6]

Capitalism Engineers World Take-over

Thus we see that Mr. Roosevelt did not care that Mr. Hiss or anyone else in his administration was a Communist for "several of the best friends I have got are Communists." It was Mr. Hiss, a member of the CFR, that advised Roosevelt to give away East Europe in fulfillment of Lenin's plan for the Communist conquest of the world.

At the close of the Second World War Japan was ready to surrender, but we continued to plead with the Russians to agree to join in the battle against Japan. Finally Stalin agreed, on the condition that we would place in Manchuria billions of dollars' worth of military aid with which the Russians could fight the Japanese. The aid was delivered and then the announcement was made that Russia had entered the war against Japan. Six days later Japan was allowed to surrender. All of those billions of dollars' worth of military aid supplied by the United States into Manchuria were never used by the Russians against Japan.

Then General George C. Marshall was sent to China to settle the war that had been raging between the Communist Chinese forces of Mao Tse-tung and the Free Chinese forces of Chiang Kai-shek. Strangely enough, Marshall demanded of Chiang that he set up a coalition government with Mao, a half-free and half-Communist regime. Chiang had seen what had happened to Poland and the other countries which had tried such a setup and would not have anything to do with it. He had been very successful in beating back Mao several times and felt that now with the Japanese out of the way he would not have any trouble beating the Communists and establishing a Free China. Little did he know that the billions of dollars of unused military aid in Manchuria would now be turned over by the Russians to Mao. Now armed with enormous quantities of modern equipment and supplies Mao was ready to launch a new offensive.

Then General Marshall did a very strange thing for a General who was supposed to be promoting freedom; he said to Chiang Kai-shek, "As Chief of Staff I armed 39 anti-Communist divisions; now with a stroke of a pen I disarm them." Thus all supplies, food, ammunition, equipment and money were cut off from the Free Chinese forces.[7]

Who was General George C. Marshall? He was a member of the CFR, the organization that had been set up as the offspring of the Secret Societies of Europe and England by "Colonel" House to establish "one-world government as dreamed of by Karl Marx."

Thus, true to the plan outlined by Lenin, the Communists took the masses of Asia, but in reality it was not taken anymore than was Russia or Eastern Europe. It was given to them by those in command.

THE FINAL STEP

The final step before taking over the United States was to ring this nation with Communist nations. The beginning of this came with the loss of Cuba to the Communist dictator Fidel Castro. How did it happen?

It began when President Eisenhower, a member of the CFR, appointed Christian Herter to be the Secretary of State. Under Herter's direction a man by the name of William Arthur Wieland was appointed director of the Caribbean Desk of the State Department. Although ambassadors to Cuba cried loudly to the State Department that Wieland was promoting a Communist to power, Christian Herter, Secretary of State, systematically ignored the reports and placed his blessings on Wieland. A Senate Internal Security Subcommittee filed a report that leaders in the State Department disregarded reports from their own department, the FBI, and the military that Castro was a Communist. Various newsmen inspired by the leadership of the renowned Edward R. Murrow covered the nation with the news that Castro was not a Communist, that he was merely a modern-day Robin Hood. Once Castro was in power he announced that he was a Communist and had been a Communist all along. Thus, through the aid and blessings of newsman Murrow and Secretary of State Christian Herter, Castro the Communist took over Cuba, just 90 miles off our own shores.

Why did Murrow and Herter deliberately ignore the intelligence reports and tell the American people and the government that Castro was not a Communist? Why did they deliberately build him up to be a hero and do everything they could to help him get in power when the State Department had been warned again and again that Castro was a Communist? Why? Because they were members of the CFR, the organization that was founded by "Colonel" House to "set up a one-world government as dreamed of by Karl Marx"; that is why!

There is no way that Communism could ever win anywhere in the world without the help of the United States. Communism has always been a failure everywhere it has been tried; whether on an experimental farm in America or in Russia, it has always failed. Before Communism took over in Russia, the Russians exported grain to the rest of Europe; but ever since then the Communists have had to import grain, in spite of the fact that millions of Russians have been shot, starved and worked to death in an effort to reduce the population. China, who once exported rice, cannot support herself and has been forced to buy grain from Canada and the United States. Cuba, who used to export thousands of tons of sugar to the rest of the world, is so hard pressed to meet her quotas she has had to ration sugar in Cuba. Communism is a failure and ever has been.

Communism can conquer nothing. No nation has ever willfully stayed under Communist rule. That is why they have to build walls to keep people in. Communism has conquered the great masses of land and people that it has because a Secret Society of the richest and most influential men in the world seek to use Communism as a tool to capture the world for them. Key tool in this Secret Society is the outer ring known as the Council on Foreign Relations. No doubt many good men belong to this organization merely to associate with what seem to them to be so many top and influential men in "the affairs of business and state"; no doubt many of these men are innocent of any malevolent intentions; no doubt they have simply been duped into coming along, just as the rest of us have, thinking that all of the mistakes and miscalculations of the State Department and the government which have allowed the Communist take-over of the world, all of this is merely an accident. However, even a gambler in Las Vegas knows that once in awhile the law of averages says you have to win one. When? When have we ever won against the Communists?

Communism has always won because there is a Secret Society composed of the world's richest and most powerful International Bankers and Capitalists who from the very beginning have financed it. It has won because through this Secret Society's Foreign Affairs Clubs throughout the world, and especially the Council on Foreign Relations in America, they have been able to take control of major government posts and deliberately engineer diplomatic blunders which have resulted in Communist victories, giving them East Europe, the masses of Asia, and now an important position just 90 miles off our own coast.

CHAPTER 6

WE WON'T HAVE TO ATTACK

WE WON'T HAVE TO ATTACK

The announced plan of the Communist take-over of the United States was based upon not having to attack. All the talk about military buildup is just so much saber rattling. To attack would cause a nuclear holocaust that would destroy everything the Big Boys want to win. They do not want to lose Chicago, New York or Dallas. They have too much invested there, and they want to keep everything intact. The plan was, you will recall, to weaken us through Socialism and economics so that we will be too weak to resist the forces of Communism and will, as they have said, "fall into their hands like overripe fruit." Let's consider these two steps-- Socialism and economics--and see just how effective this technique has been.

SOCIALISM

To most Americans the term Socialism is a nebulous word, a word without specific meaning. To the Socialist it has a specific meaning, however. It means revolution. It means the change from individual to group control. It means that society, through the State, will control everything. It is very important to realize that Russia is a Socialist state.

Today England and Sweden are Socialist states moving closer and closer to being more and more like Russia. We hear so many glowing reports about the great benefits of State-supplied housing, State-supplied hospitalization, etc., etc. Recently **U.S. News and World Report** had the facts and statistics on these great Socialistic benefits. First of all, both of these nations are nearly bankrupt and both have the highest taxation rates in the world. Second, it takes seven to eight years on a waiting list for a young couple to get a decent State-furnished apartment. It takes months and months on a waiting list to get into a State-furnished hospital to get an operation once you have stood in line for days on end to see a doctor and he has certified that you need an operation. You cannot pick your doctor. You take what you can get, and he has no more interest in you than what your number is on his form so he can be paid by the State. A recent survey of these Socialist heavens by the Gallup Poll disclosed that nearly 20 percent of the people living there would like to move to another country where they could feel free. [1]

As nations move deeper and deeper into Socialism, they become more and more of a failure--products and services become scarcer and scarcer, quality goes down, and prices and crime go up. The process has been identical in every nation where Socialism has been tried.

MORAL SOCIALISM

Modern Socialism had its beginning in 1883 with the founding of the Fabian Society in England. They began a deliberate program to change the thinking of the various Western nations. It is what we call today brainwashing and mind conditioning. They began by following ideas laid down by Adam Weishaupt. Gaining control of as many writers, journalists, newspapers, magazines, teachers, professors and preachers as they could, they began by teaching the concept that there were various individuals that had to suffer in society because there were others who would take advantage of them. This of course is true. However, what they proposed was that if they--that is, the kind and warm-hearted Socialists--were in charge of the government and the government had control of everything else, they could then eliminate these terrible social injustices.

We Won't Have to Attack

To enter in upon such sensitive grounds as an individual's rights results in tampering with his moral beliefs and convictions. Therefore, before you can convince a man that it is his moral responsibility to let the government care for everything, you first have to convince him he has no real responsibility to take care of himself. Man has to be reduced to nothing more than another animal. God has to be eliminated. In every country where Socialism gets a good foothold you will see a corresponding death of religion and a rise in crime and immorality. They first start in the seminaries. They seek to exalt the seminary instructors who downgrade the divinity of certain traditional beliefs and gradually continue until over a course of years they succeed in getting most of the clergy to doubt the reality of God and the divinity of Christ.

In 1961 the results of a survey of 100 ministerial students at eight different seminaries were released. The results were shocking--56 percent, more than half the group, did not believe that Jesus had a divine origin; only 2 percent believed in the eternal nature of man's soul, and only 1 percent believed in the literal Second Coming of Christ. [2]

How did it happen? In 1937 Dr. A.W. Beaven, former President of the Federal Council of Churches in Christ, wrote: "It is clear, it seems to me, that the greatest single influence on the life and thought of the American Church in the last 50 years was exerted by Walter Rauschenbusch." [3] Dr. Rauschenbusch was a devout and determined Socialist, a member of the Fabian Society under the leadership of the Atheist George Bernard Shaw. Said Rauschenbusch of the role of religion, "The only power that can make socialism succeed, if it is established, is religion." [4] To him the purpose of religion was to make Socialism work; through it he said man would set up the "Kingdom of God on Earth."

This is of course the dream of the Socialist--to set up a man-made utopia. To do this man must be convinced that there is no higher power than himself; he must be convinced that he has it within himself to create this utopia. Thus all religious morals must be broken down. Faith in anything above man must be destroyed. Once this is achieved the State becomes the supreme being, replacing God, and those who stand at the helm of the State become the deity of the State. It is not really so different from ancient Rome and Greece, and where are they today?

This whole view is summed up very well by one of the leading American Socialists, Arthur Schlesinger, Jr., who has written that Socialism

> ... dispensed with the absurd Christian myths of sin and damnation and believed that what shortcomings man might have were to be redeemed, not by Jesus on the Cross, but by the benevolent unfolding of history. Tolerance, free inquiry, and technology, operating in the framework of human perfectability, would in the end create a heaven on earth, a goal accounted much more sensible and wholesome than a heaven in heaven.[5]

Mr. Schlesinger is a former Presidential advisor and is a member of the CFR.

Through this approach, religion which has been the guardian of the morals has now become to a large degree the key to unlock the door to immorality. Dr. Joseph F. Fletcher, professor of ethics at Cambridge Episcopal Theological School, believes the Ten Commandments are no longer valid as originally given. He would amend them to read:

> Thou shalt not covet, ordinarily. Thou shalt not kill, ordinarily. Thou shalt not commit

We Won't Have to Attack

adultery, ordinarily. In other words, for me there are no rules--none at all. . . . anything and everything is right or wrong according to the situation.[6]

That is an example of how the leadership of some of the churches is leading the people of America down the path of immorality. This is the exact teaching of morality that is taught to the young Russian under Communist rule. What is right is what is determined to be right for the advance of the State. It is right to lie, to cheat, to steal, and to do all manner of wrong if it is for the benefit of the State. We now see this is an official policy of the Nixon Administration. They have lied and lied again, openly, about the War, about the whereabouts of government officials, especially Henry Kissinger. As long as it advances the interest of the leaders of government, it is supposed to be all right. How long? How long will we have to be deceived and abused before we as Americans can wake up and realize what is happening to us as a nation?

In the area of the press and communications the Fabians, liberals, lefties and Socialists abound, as in other fields of endeavor that have a big influence on the minds of the public. The Socialists began long ago to capture the schools which were turning out the professional people that would dominate that area. Then they use their behind-the-scenes influence to be sure that those who have graduated from the left-leaning schools and who put out the right kind, or should I say the left kind, of copy get all of the good jobs. As an example of how just one liberal institution can influence a whole field, we will note that graduates of the Socialist-oriented Columbia School of Journalism now include 45 newspaper publishers, 152 newspaper editors, and 71 magazine editors. No doubt these people are talented and well educated; however, such a remarkable record of success may also indicate that they have an inside track to the top because they know just how to interpret the news. Nowadays students in the field of journalism are taught to do "interpretive reporting," which is of course just a trick in semantics, meaning "slant the news." Always to the left of the page, of course.

Nationally syndicated columnist and Pulitzer Prize winner Morrie Ryskind has written:

> If I return to the subject of "interpretive reporting," it is because it remains the biggest psychological weapon in the armament of the Liberal Establishment. In the bright lexicon of revolution--and that's what we're going through, whether we realize it or not--the news is not nearly as important as the manner in which it is filtered down to the public. And no item is too small to be passed without going through the screening process. After all, war is war. [7]

In this great battle the news seems to be distorted more than reported and tinted instead of just printed. Thus the nation was fed the propaganda that Mao is a simple Chinese peasant bent on land reforms, out to help the little man in that great big country. Then AFTER he established his power we learned that he IS a Communist after all. When Castro was seeking his power in Cuba, the newsmen almost unanimously declared again and again that he was NOT a Communist. Then AFTER he was in power we learned that he really IS a Communist.

Can we honestly believe that ALL those newsmen are really so stupid that they cannot tell a Communist Revolution when they see one? If so, we are in tough shape when it comes to newsmen, and we really can't

We Won't Have to Attack

rely on the accuracy or dependability of their "interpretive reporting." Since we must conclude that just on the basis of the law of averages someone would have seen through the big lie, we must also conclude that-- Yes, Virginia, there is a Conspiracy.

This Conspiracy has infiltrated the schools, the churches, and the communications media. Through them the conspirators have spread the great lie that morality as we have known it is no longer valid; we have been sold the idea that Communists are not Communists and that Socialism will create a utopia for everyone in the United States. Meanwhile we become weaker and weaker with ever-rising divorce, illegitimacy, venereal disease, and crime of every description. As the home is split apart, the youth become more and more discontent and less and less viable as a source of national strength. Conditioned by years of clever interpretive news reports, Americans sit as though numb, watching a major Communist power move into a World Government with our approval and push out our long-time friend and ally, Free China. Through all of these things we have as Khrushchev predicted become so weakened that we not only do not resist the advance of Communism but actually seem to roll out the welcome mat for our own enslavement.

POLITICAL SOCIALISM

As the moral Socialists poured out their propaganda in the schools and churches and media, we Americans began to accept more and more Socialism in politics. We have allowed the installment of boards and commissions and rules and regulations that rob us of pure basic fundamental rights of freedom.

LOSS OF PRIVACY

In violation of your Constitutional rights you are

forced in the name of law to reveal your income and expenses and to pay a tax on the net amount each year. Each time you do this, you incriminate yourself, for if the government should disallow any of your claims you are subject to severe penalties. This is in direct violation of the Fifth Amendment to the Constitution of the United States which states you do not have to divulge any information which may tend to incriminate you. In addition you are granted the right to the privacy of your books and records by the Fourth Amendment of the Constitution. The collection of income taxes violates your Constitutionally guaranteed freedoms. The second point in a 10-point plan to weaken free nations as outlined in the Communist Manifesto calls for the establishment of a graduated income tax. Thus we have subscribed to one of the 10 points that weakens free nations as outlined in the Communist Manifesto, in direct violation of the rights and freedoms granted in the Constitution. [8]

SELF-INCRIMINATION

Today you must register all handguns and ammunition even though the Constitution of the land specifically states that citizens have a right to keep and bear arms. When you register a weapon, if that weapon is found to have been used in any type of crime, whether by you or not, you have become incriminated and involved. The information you gave by registering caused you to incriminate yourself, a direct violation of the Fifth Amendment of the Constitution. The first step in crushing resistance in any nation taken over by the Communists is the registration and subsequent confiscation of weapons. This is exactly what occurred in the Communist take-over of East Europe. [9]

WORTHLESS CURRENCY

Although the Constitution stipulates in Article 1, Section 10, Clause 1, that only gold and silver coin is to be legal tender for all debts, the government no longer issues either gold or silver coins. Although up until 1950 paper currency bore the promise of redemption in lawful money (this promise no longer appears on the Federal Reserve Notes we use as currency), any attempt to redeem this paper currency for lawful money in gold and silver as stipulated in the Constitution will result in failure. There is no lawful money in either gold or silver. This is part of the Communist plan to weaken free nations. Here is how it works.

When the government allows money to be placed into circulation without having any gold or silver backing it, it is worthless and dilutes the purchasing power of all money that is already in circulation. When private individuals do this, it is called counterfeiting; when the government does it, it is called inflation--but it still robs people of their wealth. For example, let's suppose there is one thousand dollars in circulation. Then the government puts one hundred additional dollars in circulation, but it has no backing in either gold or silver. This would then dilute the value of the thousand dollars in circulation by 10 percent. It would be the same as robbing the people who had the thousand dollars of 10 percent of their money. The founding fathers understood this; that is why they stipulated that all legal tender had to be in gold and silver, to keep the politicians honest and to prevent them from using the scheme of official counterfeiting known as inflation.

Since 1940 the government has put so much inflated currency in circulation that, according to the American Institute of Economic Research, it has robbed the people of over $700 billion. The Department of Labor states that inflation, which is official counterfeiting, has caused the value of the dollar (which if we use 1940 as a base year at 100 cents) to drop to 30 cents by 1970. Lenin knew that free nations could be broken down in this manner and stated:

> The best way to destroy the Capitalist System is to debauch the currency. By a continuing process of inflation, governments can confiscate, secretly and unobserved an important part of the wealth of their citizens. [10]

While Constitutionally illegal income taxes have multiplied 35 times, the value of unconstitutional money has dropped 70 percent, robbing you and your fellow citizens of the fruit of your labors and denying you a profit on your savings. You have already lost the freedom of a stable currency.

STATE-CONTROLLED COMMERCE

Our red-blooded forefathers were so angered by the King of England's imposing a few pennies tax on their tea that they threw the stuff in the ocean at the Boston Tea Party. Now we Americans are so docile that we allow the government to confiscate 30 percent of everything we produce in the form of taxes. Then to add insult to injury we have now allowed the government to take away our freedom to buy and sell on a free market. Wages and prices are now set by the government. You cannot pay less than a certain amount for a man or woman's wages and you cannot pay more than a certain set amount. You cannot sell your goods or services for more than the government tells you to sell it for. You cannot earn profits higher than the government tells you you can earn. Thus you have already lost the freedom to hire, to buy, to sell, and to earn.

We Won't Have to Attack

If you are in the transportation industry, you can operate only on those highways and carry that particular type of cargo that the government tells you you can, and of course at what rate they stipulate. If you are in the farming business, you cannot plant and grow what the government does not tell you you can plant and grow, even if you intend to use it yourself.

Violation of the government's directives will result in severe penalties. So you see, my friend, one by one our freedoms are being stripped away and the government is taking over regulation of our lives.

FINANCIAL BONDAGE

Through the power of taxation the government has been confiscating more and more of our wealth. Now they use that wealth to support financially the police, the schools, the hospitals, the cities, and state agencies. First comes the money, for three and four years. The money flows like a fountain; the recipients are not prepared for this great largess. They ask for help, for guidance in the use of the money, but are told that none is available. Naturally this results in excesses and abuses. Then the worst cases are isolated and the public spotlight is turned on. This demonstrates that the government must lay down some guidelines for the use of this money, to protect the taxpayers' investment. By now the budgets of the agencies involved are so heavily dependent on the handout they willingly accept the controls rather than lose the money. Year by year the guidelines are strengthened until they are not guidelines any longer but controls. Through this method the citizens of this nation are fast losing all control over health care, welfare, police, education, city, county and state government.

REPUBLICANS AND DEMOCRATS

As was stated at the beginning of this book, Norman Thomas, six-time Presidential candidate on the Socialist ticket, retired because he said that Republicans and Democrats were doing such a good job of Socializing the country he no longer felt needed. Time after time the people go to the polls to vote in a change. Americans do not like all of this Socialism. They want to win their wars, they want to defeat Communism, they want their taxes eliminated, they want the budget balanced, they want the government out of debt, they want their privacy respected, they want the streets to be safe from crime, they want to be able to earn what they can without the government telling them or their employer what they can and must pay, they want open and free trade without the government interfering. Americans want what America has always stood for. That is why when Mr. Nixon promised in 1968 to give it to them they believed him and voted for him. Americans wanted the Conservative type of government he promised.

But what happened? Mr. Nixon reversed his stand. As Harvard Professor John Kenneth Gailbraith, a professed Socialist, has stated it:

> Certainly the least predicted development under the Nixon Administration was this great new thrust to Socialism. One encounters people who still aren't aware of it. Others must be rubbing their eyes, for certainly the portents seemed all to the contrary. [11]

Indeed all of Mr. Nixon's campaign rhetoric did seem to portend a Conservative type of administration. The sudden shift to the left has left many people rubbing their eyes and wondering what happened.

But it is really not so hard to figure out. Economic

policies and measures were employed at the outset of the Administration that ran the country into a serious economic crisis, a crisis that was deliberately engineered as an excuse to push us deep into Socialistic policies. According to Mr. Gailbraith,

> Mr. Nixon is probably not a great reader of Marx, but his advisors Drs. Burns, Shultz and McCracken are excellent scholars who know him well and could have brought the President abreast and it is beyond denying that the **crisis that aided the rush into Socialism was engineered by the Administration.** [12] (Emphasis the author's.)

It is thus clear that we have been deliberately engineered into more and more Socialism.

It must be born in mind that Richard M. Nixon is a former member of the Council on Foreign Relations and that his chief advisors, Drs. Kissinger, Burns and McCracken, as well as over a hundred other of the top members of the Nixon Administration, are currently members of that group. You will recall that the CFR was established by "Colonel" House, whose goal it was to establish a "one-world government as dreamed of by Karl Marx." Now we find Dr. Gailbraith, a member of the CFR along with Drs. Burns and McCracken, telling us that they are disciples of Karl Marx and that it is their influence that has brought the President deeper into Socialism. It makes no difference which major party is elected to office. During the past 40 years the CFR has managed to grab the most powerful and influential posts in both Democratic and Republican administrations.

Noted columnist for the **New York Times**, James Reston, a member of the Council on Foreign Relations and one who generally knows what is going on on the inside, had this to say about Mr. Nixon's sudden embracing of the Communist Chinese:

> Nixon would obviously like to preside over the creation of a "new world order" and believes HE sees an opportunity to do so in the last twenty months of his first term. [13]

You will recall that the purpose of the CFR is to establish that "New World Order" of Socialism as dreamed of by Karl Marx; you will also recall that establishing a "New World Order" was the goal of Weishaupt and the Illuminati. Mr. Nixon when a member of Congress submitted a bill to establish a World Police Force. He has gone on record as establishing the power of the United Nations to such an extent that it will rule the world. The list of quotations and examples we could cite illustrating Mr. Nixon's rapid move to the left is very long and very impressive but sufficient evidence has been introduced here to illustrate that we have politically moved deep into the waters of Socialism. We have moved faster under the leadership of Republican Richard Nixon than we did under many supposedly liberal Democratic Presidents. The main point is to remember Khrushchev's warning that we would be given small doses of Socialism until one day we would wake up to find that we already have Communism.

Khrushchev's statement said "we" will keep feeding you small doses of Socialism. Who is "we"? We have never had a Communist Congressman or Senator or President. Yet we as a nation keep getting marched down the path of Communist-Socialism by the administrations of both Democrats and Republicans. The one thing they have all had in common has been members of their administrations with increasing numbers and importance who are members of the CFR.

We Won't Have to Attack

When we realize that Communism is merely a branch of a more secretive conspiracy; when we realize that the Rockefellers, for example, own a corporation which researches the U.S. Patent Office and sells the information to the Russians, own oil interest in Russia, have made business investments in Russia, paid for the CFR building and land and have been its chief financial backer, have aided and assisted in the bringing of leading Communists to the United States, and donated the land for the United Nations Building--the organization they hope will one day rule the world--that David Rockefeller, head of one of the world's leading banks, vacations in Russia, one such vacation mysteriously preceding the firing of Khrushchev, it is not too hard to figure out who "we" is. "We" is the members both in and out of government that ascribe to the concept of a "New World Order" as laid down first by Adam Weishaupt and later restated by Karl Marx. They may or may not be members of any formal group or organization. Some are open in their actions; others are secretive. Some are aware of what they are doing; some are not. But all are working consciously or unconsciously, openly or secretively, for the establishment of a "New World Order."

ECONOMICS

The second step in Khrushchev's boast was to weaken us through economics till we would fall into their hands. Karl Marx laid down the premise by which this was to be done.

In the second plank for destroying free nations he stated that a heavy graduated income tax should be established. This allows the people of the nation to be taxed with an ever-increasing taxation policy until they are left destitute. It has become virtually impossible for anyone to hold a job and get ahead. The tax burden is so heavy upon the poor and middle class that they have no possibility of being secure and happy. They have no way of establishing a state of independence. They become dependent upon the government for their welfare when sick and old. Whenever people are dependent upon someone that other person becomes their boss and their master. They are afraid to insist upon certain basic fundamental principles in government even though they know they are right because they fear the loss of income and security from government programs. Thus through taxation they become their own worst enemy.

However, the fifth plank in the plan by Marx is the one that really allows the government to get a stranglehold on the people and so weaken the nation that it falls into the hands of the "New World Order" without the enemy having to attack. That plank calls for the establishment of a national bank that can control all of the currency and credit of the nation and thus control all of the economic life of the nation.

In the year 1913 through the behind-the-scenes work of "Colonel" House, the man that founded the CFR, a national bank such as Marx outlined was established. The bank is known as the Federal Reserve Bank. It is partially owned by the government and partially by private stockholders. Those private stockholders are the same wealthy International Financiers that control the CFR and the other Secret Societies. The Federal Reserve Bank is operated and controlled entirely by private bankers. It is true that the President does appoint and the Senate does ratify seven members to be directors of the bank. These men serve for a 14-year term and are completely autonomous in their actions. The United States government has no control over the Federal Reserve and its actions, in spite of the fact that the Federal Reserve controls virtually all of the

We Won't Have to Attack

currency in circulation in this nation today as well as the manipulation of all the credit in existence.

NATION CONTROLLED BY A FEW

Woodrow Wilson was financed into office by the Super-Rich; and acting as public-spirited individuals, they assisted him by giving him some of their best brains as advisors. Chief among them was "Colonel" House, who used his influence to get President Wilson to support the Federal Reserve Act. After the nation was stuck with the Federal Reserve System, President Wilson came to realize their great power and made this very revealing statement:

> We have come to be one of the worst ruled, one of the most completely controlled and dominated governments in the civilized world-- no longer a government by free opinion, no longer a government by conviction and the vote of the majority, but a government by the opinion and duress of small groups of dominant men.[14]

Much to his obvious sorrow President Wilson came to realize that the Federal Reserve Banking Act had set up a giant monopoly that allowed only a few to control the credit and currency of the entire nation. As a result, he said that we had "government by the opinion and duress of small groups of dominant men." In addition, President Wilson said that a nation such as ours "is controlled by its system of credit. Our system of credit is concentrated...in the hands of a few men."[15] Earlier President Grover Cleveland had said, "Those who control the economy of the nation control the nation."[16]

The small group of men that control the economy of the nation, the group that President Wilson was referring to, is the Federal Reserve Board and those behind the scenes that placed them there. An example of their extreme power in controlling the nation was demonstrated in August of 1962 before the Joint Economic Committee of Congress in sworn testimony by Mariner Eccles, chairman of the Federal Reserve Board. Chairman Rep. Wright Patman asked him, "Is it not a fact that the Federal Reserve system has more power than either the Congress or the President?" Eccles responded, "In the field of money and credit, yes."[17] As further evidence of the superior power of the Federal Reserve over the officers of the government, I will cite the fact that in 1969 the Federal Reserve raised their interest rate causing the economy to shrink the following year by $20 billion. When Secretary of the Treasury David Kennedy was asked by U.S. News and World Report if he approved of the Federal Reserve doing such a thing, he responded, "It's not my job to approve or disapprove. It is the action of the Federal Reserve."[18]

Thus by admissions of both members of the government and the Federal Reserve we see that the Federal Reserve is in matters of finance superior to our elected and appointed representatives in government. As Rothschild said so many years ago, "Give me control of a nation's currency and I care not who makes its laws." As Reginald McKenna, once Chancellor of the Exchanger of the Bank of England stated in 1924, "They who control the credit of the nation direct the policy of governments and hold in the hollow of their hands the destiny of the people."[19]

SAPPING OUR STRENGTH

With the ability to control the credit of the nation the Federal Reserve is in the position to cause the economy to remain stable, to become insolvent, to stagnate, or to leap forward. If the Federal Reserve should choose to expand the supply of paper currency in great excess of the gold or silver reserves it has--this means printing paper money without anything backing it, called inflation--they could continue the process until the money was worthless and the economy failed. Unfortunately, they have done this. Today they have expanded the amount of paper money in ratio to the amount of real wealth behind it till there is less than 4 cents backing each paper bill.

The foreign nations of the world no longer have the same value and respect for American currency they once had. This is because they know that it is only paper and has no real wealth behind it. These nations are afraid that we are going to go bankrupt and they will be left holding a lot of worthless pieces of paper. Many shrewd and carefully observant businessmen become afraid of the same thing happening, so each wants to get a bigger and bigger price for doing business with this money. The idea is that if you can get enough of this money you will be able to lay claim to enough of the assets of the nation to get back what you should for the product or service you produced. However, as the money becomes more and more worthless as the Federal Reserve continues to make more and more of it available without any backing, people begin to lose all faith in the currency. Eventually it becomes so worthless no one will accept it in trade.

In the spring of 1972 the Federal Reserve is expanding the issuance of inflationary paper money at the rate of 11 percent. This is causing people everywhere to lose faith in the American currency. Soon even price controls will not be able to maintain the economy. This inflation has robbed the American people of more than $700 billion of their wealth since 1940.

It was Lenin who said that this was the best way to destroy free nations because it could be done secretly and not one man in a million would be able to detect it until it was too late. Thus through inflation we have been robbed of hundreds of billions of dollars of our true wealth, the strength of the people has been sapped, and we have been left with worthless pieces of paper. This always leads to an economic crash.

NO FREEDOM IN ECONOMIC CRASH

When someone has a gun held at your head, you do not have any freedom. When the economy of a nation goes broke and you have no money to buy anything with, when you have no job and you have lost much of what you have paid for because you cannot finish paying for it, you have lost much of your freedom. You become dependent upon the government to re-establish some type of economy so that you can eat and live. The degree to which you are dependent upon the government to save you is the degree to which you have lost your freedom. When the situation becomes bad enough, you are willing to accept any kind of government. You begin to believe that it would be "better to be red than dead." You will be willing to sell your pride and self-respect and your freedoms for a little food for you and your family.

Those who have been planning this world take-over have known and understood this principle for a long time. They know that a free and financially independent people such as the people of the United States traditionally have been would never accept the tyranny and dictatorship of a Communist type of government. But if they could get control of the nation's Central Bank and issue the currency, through a process of ever-increasing inflation, they could rob the citizens of their

We Won't Have to Attack

wealth and bankrupt the nation. Then when the people are in that awful situation of destitution, they would be willing to give up their freedoms and surrender to the "New World Order" the conspirators wish to place upon them.

ECONOMICALLY DESTROYED

We have through that process been economically destroyed. Today we have been forced to devalue the dollar once, and there are continually mounting pressures to devalue again. Meanwhile the government continues to go deeper and deeper into debt, and inflationary currency is being produced and inflationary credit is being extended to such an extent that the nation is like an overinflated balloon about to break. The balance of payments to other nations continues to be out of balance, and this gives them more and more power to force us into national bankruptcy. The government continues to roll forward in a massive spending spree. The Gross National Product is slowing in its growth rate, and taxes and debt are rising at an ever-increasing pace. Thus we are heading on a collision course with an economic disaster in the very near future.

All that will be necessary to bring this about is for the Federal Reserve to raise their interest rate, the rate known as the Discount Interest Rate. This will cause the banks to call for the payment of all short-term and call loans, and this will have the effect of shrinking the economy. When people in business cannot use money to expand their business and to hire other people but have to pay the money to the bank before they had planned to, it causes unemployment to go up. With fewer people working there are fewer paychecks to cash and spend; fewer things are bought. This causes other people to be put out of work and starts a cycle that continues to pick up steam. Once this reaches a certain point, the stock market begins to be flooded by people who must sell their investments and savings in stocks and bonds in order to eat and pay their bills. As there are more sellers than buyers, the prices start to fall, falling faster and faster until there is what is known as a stock market crash. At that point the nation begins to go into a nightmare known as a depression.

The economy of the nation has been so effectively destroyed through inflation and the dissipation of our national treasury that any contraction of the credit will have a rapid and devastating effect upon the economy resulting in a very deep and serious depression. Any error in judgment, any miscalculation on the part of those in control of the economic affairs of the nation could start us on the road to economic ruin. So complete has been the destruction of the integrity of our economic situation that it is no longer a question of if we will have a depression but of when. It was planned this way from the beginning; as Khrushchev said, "We will weaken your economy until you fall into our hands like an overripe fruit." For a detailed explanation of the economic deterioration of the nation see the author's book, **How To Prepare for the Coming Crash.**

THE COMMUNIST CONSTITUTION

We have seen that the Super-Rich have worked their way into government through the CFR and have taken control of the foreign policy of the nation, carefully guiding the country into decisions and actions which have been beneficial to the advance of Communism which they have employed to conquer the world for them. Now we see that through their control of the Federal Reserve System and their influence on men in government they have guided the economic policies of our nation on a downhill course until we are so weak

We Won't Have to Attack

that we are no longer a financially solvent nation, strong and independent and capable of leading the rest of the world. This is the exact position the Super-Rich have been working for; now they are prepared to serve us the Coup de grace.

In the midst of a deliberately planned and carefully timed depression, when the nation is starving, and rioting and looting and murder have convinced most people that something was wrong with our form of government that it would let such a terrible thing happen, we will see introduced as a solution to our problems a new constitution. This constitution will set up a new form of government that will promise to do away with the threat of such a thing recurring. This new constitution and form of government will have built into it extensive and rigid procedures of planning and control to prevent such things from ever happening again. It will not be called one, but it will be a Communist Constitution.

Overnight the United States of America will be turned into another Communist-type nation. Freedom will be gone! In its place will be controls and strict regulations--you will not be able to work, eat or live without permission to do so. Violators of the regulations and controls will be shipped off to slave labor camps or shot on the spot as an example to others who might be tempted to violate the rules.

IT'S ALREADY HERE

To many people this sounds like a pipe dream, the overworked imagination of a reactionary, and would be except for the fact that it has all happened according to plan. It is not speculation concerning something in the far-off future. We are talking about history--documented facts and figures, names and dates, times and places. It has happened.

Even the new constitution for this nation is past history. It was drawn up over a six-year period and published in the fall of 1970 by the Center for the Study of Democratic Institutions located in Santa Barbara, California. It was financed by the Super-Rich; the Ford Foundation alone put up $15 million. The prime authors of this new constitution have also prepared a constitution for a "New World Order," a world government, since the United Nations only has a charter and not a constitution. In fact, these authors have stated that one of the main reasons we need a new constitution is the "old" one does not cover world government. These dedicated souls that poured their hearts into this new constitution sacrificed their all at salaries ranging from $20,000 to $50,000 a year to write this new constitution. It is obvious that once again we see it is the work of the Super-Rich. A careful review of the individuals involved and the new constitution itself can be found in the author's book, **The Plot To Replace the Constitution.**

This Communist Constitution does away with the concept of "innocent till proven guilty": it places the burden of proof on the accused. It does away with things like trial by jury and replaces the judicial system with a tribunal of judges like the system they have in Russia. It completely eliminates God from all public life and bans Him from government--no more dedicatory prayers, no more chaplains, and soon, as in Russia, no more religion. Freedom for the average man is soon to be a thing of the past in America if the Super-Rich have their way.

TIMING THE BIG SWITCH

In the announced plans of the authors of this new constitution, it is to be adopted as a result of a national crisis. Obviously, the only way they are ever going to get the American people to give up their freedoms and to adopt their new constitution is under the duress of a national crisis. It is equally obvious that the one thing completely within the power and scope of the Super-Rich is the manipulation of the economy and the establishment of a depression that will leave people cold, naked, hungry and starving. Under these conditions even strong people will be willing to accept a new constitution in exchange for some food and heat and clothing.

When we study the economy, we see that it has been manipulated till we are on the verge of an economic collapse at the very moment. All that it will take to bring this about is for the Federal Reserve to raise the Discount Rate. This will cause the stock market to begin to slide downhill, creating a recession. At that point the Super-Rich can precipitate an overnight crash at any time that it suits them by simply dumping large blocks of stock on the market at one time. They can do this through the Open Market Committee of the Federal Reserve or through the dumping of stocks held by two or three of the major stockholding corporations controlled by the Morgans, Fords, Rockefellers, Schiffs, and other such Super-Rich dynasties.

This will most likely occur in the fall of the year or in early winter when it will work the greatest hardships on the people of the nation. It could occur as early as 1972 or 1973. It may not happen till 1975, but **it will happen!** You can count on it. Everything they have planned up until now has gone off according to plan, and there is no reason to believe that they will not deliver the final blow after all these years of preparation. You can also believe that **it will occur before 1976**, since they want to celebrate May 1, 1976, which will be the 200th anniversary of the founding of the Secret Society with a victory over America and the establishment of a world government.

CHAPTER 7

KNOWLEDGE IS NOT ENOUGH

To know that there is a Conspiracy to rule the world, to know that the economy is failing, to know that there has been a new constitution written, to know that we are going to be coerced into a new form of government that will rob us of our rights is not enough. Knowledge is only power when it is translated into direct and positive action. It is no longer a question of saving this principle or this freedom. We are in a battle that can only end in one thing--either total freedom of the individual or total slavery.

If you wish to end up a slave of the State with some Super-Rich ruler who thinks that he and his fellows have all the brains and they can tell you what to think, what to wear, what to eat, where you will work and live and where you can go, how many if any children you can have--if this is the way you want to end up, then forget what you have read and don't become involved. But if you want to be able to think for yourself, read what you want, study what you want, write what you want, paint what you want, sing what you want, say what you want, worship the way you want, work where you want, have as many children as you want, go where you want, earn what you want, save what you want, spend what you want-- if you want that kind of life, you must become involved and you must become involved now.

POWER INVOLVEMENT

As these lines go to press, it is mid-1972; the precious sands of time are slipping through the hourglass of freedom. Direct action and confrontation economically and politically between the forces of freedom and Communism will have their face-to-face showdown in the United States within the next one to five years. It cannot be forestalled because the economic position of the United States is so far gone that an economic collapse cannot be detained any longer than that. Those who value and cherish their political freedoms must move and they must move now--not to write to their representative who will ignore their letter, or to sign some petition to Congress that will be ignored like the largest one that was ever presented to them with one-and-three-quarter million signatures by the John Birch Society. Congress will not respond, the City Council will not respond, the County Commission will not respond, the State Legislature will not respond, the Governor and the President will not respond to such mild forms of action. They have amassed so much power and wealth behind them, they have ignored us the people for so long and gotten away with it that they no longer pay any real attention to us.

There is only one way to change things. Only one way! That is to recruit our own candidates and put them into office ourselves--men and women we the people have selected, backed, worked for, financed and put into office--men and women who owe their allegiances to us the people, the people who put them into office. Those who do not respond to our wishes should be recalled by petition and vote and replaced by those who represent the will of the people of the nation, not those who do the will of the Special Interest Groups. We must become directly involved in the electorial process; this is where the power is. This is power involvement.

ORGANIZED EFFORT

Most Americans do not like what is going on. They do not like the big giveaways. They do not like the social reforms that do not work and cost more and more and breed more and more welfare. They do not believe the slick Madison Ave. advertising techniques that try to sell us on Socialist-Communist welfarism through government intervention in the lives of private individuals. They do not like the higher and higher taxes that keep the poor in a state of perpetual poverty with inflation that prevents them from being able to save and get ahead and pushes the cost of everything out of their reach and fills their heart and mind with despair and disappointment and destroys their energy and ambition because of the hopelessness of their condition, a condition which has been deliberately brought on by the economic policies of the Socialistically oriented government.

While Mr. & Mrs. Average American may not be a match for the clever words of the intellectually educated sophisticates, all of the words do not destroy their commonsense which tells them that it is wrong, unworkable and un-American. Time and again they have gone to the polls and voted for a man that lied, a man that promised to end the crime, to stop the burgeoning welfarism, to stop the no-win wars, to reduce the taxes, the budget and the inflation, just as Mr. Nixon promised in 1968. But he lied to the American people and has failed to keep any of his commitments. In fact, he, as with all of his predecessors for the past 40 years, has done exactly the opposite and has increased all of the things that he promised to eliminate. Why? Simply because he was not the candidate of the people. He was promoted and financed by the Big Boys, the Super-Rich, the Special Interest Groups; and the same is true of every other major candidate. Time and time again the public has sensed this. Over and over you hear the lament: But who will I vote for? I don't like any of them.

The people are not fooled. They know what is right and they know what they want, but the two major parties are controlled by the Big Boys and the only candidates the people have had the opportunity to vote for are the ones the Power People want voted for. But the people of this nation are not happy with American politics. They want their own party with their own candidates. But as individuals they can do nothing unless they become organized and pool their energies and resources. If the American people would do this, they could take back their nation from the professionals and once again we could have a nation of citizen statesmen, a nation of freedom for all, a nation of peace and prosperity.

The Big Boys know this, and so they have organized a group called Common Cause. It is financed by the Rockefellers and the Morgans, the Watsons, the Schiffs, and all of the other Big Boys that finance and control the Republicans and the Democrats. Then they have added the Madison Avenue touch to convince us that Common Cause is the party of the people. It is no such thing; it is simply another maneuver on the part of the Super-Rich to cause us to relax and feel that there is a political movement that is for the people and has the interest of the people at heart. Yet, everything Common Cause group proposes is more and more big government, more and more boards and panels and regulations, more and more loss of freedom to protect us.

We need protection all right, but it is not protection from our inability to make intelligent decisions. It is protection from the Super-Rich Power People that we need. We must become involved in an organization, our own political organization free from the taint and control of the Big Boys. Certainly we don't want to step into the trap of Common Cause which has been created by them for us to think that it is our political party. The Big Boys have done this because they know that we the people are not satisfied and they know that we may just get organized and take it all away from them on the very eve of their plans for the final victory.

SUPPORT LIBERTY LOBBY

You must act now to unite your strength with others who are already organized. Of all the organizations available we feel that Liberty Lobby stands out head and shoulders above the others in actually doing something constructive about our problems. We feel that they are the most honest and effective organization to fight the conspiracy which exists today. Colonel Dahl, who heads this organization, was the first man to really expose the true nature of the conspiracy to destroy our freedoms. The organization which he heads is far more effective in bringing about changes in Washington than any other organization we know of. This organization is growing very rapidly and is developing some marvelous programs to help you protect your freedoms. Just as we are throwing our support behind Liberty Lobby, so are many other Freedom organizations. It is time to unite on the Freedom Front and close ranks on the enemy. There is no better way that we know of than to unite in Liberty Lobby. You will be kept informed not only of what is happening, but what you can do as an individual, and what the Lobby itself is doing. They will keep you informed as to what your senators and representatives are doing. You will be on top of things and have a chance to participate in the many programs which they are sponsoring with increasing frequency. As more and more people support this great organization with money and effort it will become more and more powerful as the voice of the people, and more and more effective in its operation. Write to them and ask how you can join with them in the fight to preserve our Constitution. Their address is:

Liberty Lobby, 300 Independence Avenue S.E., Washington, D.C. 20003

Unite on the Freedom Front--join Liberty Lobby!

THE STRENGTH OF AMERICA

In less than 200 years America has become the greatest nation the world has ever known. It was made great not by the rich and the learned men who came here from the other nations of the earth. It was made great and mighty and noble by the ordinary people who came here as the outcasts, in many instances the poor and the downtrodden, the tradesman, the shopkeeper, the farmer, the laborer, the prisoner and the debtor. In the climate of freedom each contributed his best and each could keep the rewards of his labors. It was the ordinary people--the bicycle mechanics--that gave us the great aeronautics industry. It was a man thrown out of school in the third grade because he was too stupid to learn anything that gave us the electric light, the phonograph, and the movies. It was the genius of the common man--Yankee ingenuity--that has made America great. It was the courage of ordinary men that fought at Valley Forge with bare and bleeding feet in the winter snows who defeated the mighty British Army. It was a humble man, a dirt farmer up from the sod and mud and log cabins, a political failure, that stepped forward to lead the nation back from a civil war to greatness by his outstanding example. The strength of America lies in her people, the ordinary people.

It was the Super-Rich that held back the progress of Europe and Asia for so long; and now they want to rule after such a dismal record. It was the intellectuals who taught at the universities that denied that the sun was the center of our universe; it was the learned that denied the world was round. Thus has it ever been that

Winning the Battle for Freedom

the common man has led the way to truth and progress. Now the very ones who have been responsible for leading the world in darkness for centuries want the opportunity to lead us back again. As Thomas Jefferson said, the only safe repository for freedom is in the hands of the people.

The brains and the rich have ever been for subjugation and domination of the people. Now they have developed their most comprehensive and effective attack. It is now a battle between you and them. You are the strength of America. Divided we the people will fall, united together we will stand. Shoulder to shoulder we can be united on the political front to defeat the power of the rich and brainy ones that intend to rule over us. We can wipe out the income tax, the Federal Reserve in its present form, do away with the phoney National Debt, and eliminate fraudulant and failing social programs. We can become militarily strong so that no nation will ever dare to attack us, and we can stop helping others economically so that they can become strong enough to do that. We can try our spies and traitors and stop betraying our strength and positions to our sworn enemies. We can protect the innocent and punish the guilty and stop crime in the streets and restore peace and safety to our nation and make the streets of big cities once again safe to walk in.

It is your nation; it belongs to you. If you love it, you will not stand idly by and watch it destroyed and taken over by the Conspiracy to rule the world. You will join with your fellow Americans in **Liberty Lobby, 300 Independence Ave. S.E., Washington, D.C.**, to preserve your rights and freedoms. If you do not, no one else will. America's future? **It's up to you!!!**

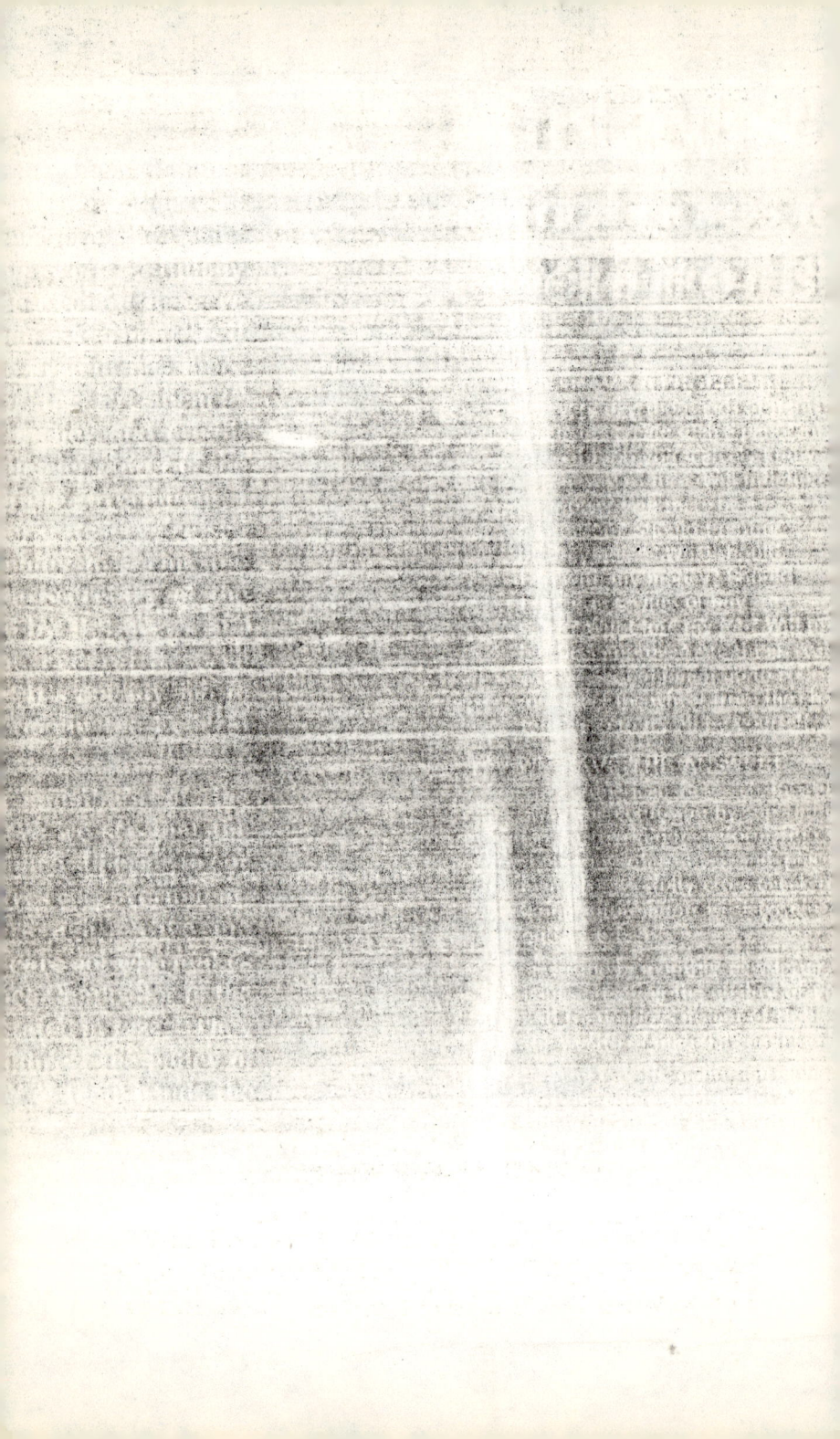

BIBLIOGRAPHY
CHAPTER 1
1. p. 16, H.L. Hunt, **Fabians Fight Freedom**.
2. p. 320, Ezra Taft Benson, **An Enemy Hath Done This**.
3. Norman Thomas, "Democratic Socialism," **Socialist Party Pamphlet, 1953**.
4. Oct. 19, 1962, **Cleveland Plain Dealer**.
5. p. 235, John M. Keynes, **The Economic Consequences of the Peace**.
6. p. 240, **Ibid**.
7. Vol. 3, No. 5, **The Center Magazine**, Center for the Study of Democratic Institutions.
8. p. 77, Cleon Skousen, **Law & Order Magazine**, March 1971.

CHAPTER 3
1. p. 172, Curtis Dall, F.D.R., **My Exploited Father-in-Law**.
2. p. 325, Caroll Quigley, **Tragedy and Hope**.
3. p. 84, John Robinson, **Proofs of a Conspiracy**.
4. Marquis de Luchet, "Essai sur la Secte des Illumines," French Archives.
5. p. 364, M. Benjamin Fabre, **Eques a Capite Galeato**.
6. See State Department Publication 2860.
7. p. 78, Nesta Webster, **World Revolution**.
8. p. 79, **Ibid**.
9. p. 520, George Washington, Vol. 20, **The Writings of George Washington**, Gov. Printing Office.
10. p. 74, Vol 1, Thomas Jefferson, **The Jefferson Cycolpedia**.
11. pp. 246, H.S. Kenan, **The Federal Reserve Bank**.
12. p. 52-53, Vol, V, Roy P. Basler, ed., **The Collected Works of Abraham Lincoln**.
13. p. 246, Kenan, **The Federal Reserve Bank, Op. cit**.
14. pp. 367-368, Gougenot des Mousseaux, **Le Juif**.
15. p. 2, Chevalier de Malet, **Recherches politiques et historiques**.
16. ii, 49, 248, James Guillaume, **Documents et souvenirs de l'Internationale**.
17. p. 528b P. Deschamps, **Les Societes Secretes**.
18. p. 24, James Guillaume, **Karl Marx, pan-Germaniste**.
19. p. 25, **Ibid**.
20. pp. 26-27, Edmond Laskine, **l'Internationale et le Pan-Germanisme**.
21. p. 9, Guillaume, **Documents, Op. cit**.
22. p. 24, Louis Enault, **Paris brule par la Commune**.
23. p. 167, Laskine, **l'Internationale, Op. cit**.
24. p. 268, Nesta Webster, **Secret Societies**.
25. xxvi, 752, Marlon, article on the Internationale, in the **Nouvelle Revue**.
26. i, 103, Guillaume, **Documents, Op. cit**.
27. Aug. 2, 1920, quoted by M. Brunet, Socialist deputy for Charleroi, in a speech in London, England.
28. Feb. 8, 1920 edition of the **Illustrated Sunday Herald**.

CHAPTER 4
1. pp. 96-97, W.B. Vennard, **The Federal Reserve Hoax**.
2. i, 80, 139 notes, Guillaume, **Documents, Op. cit**.
3. p. 81, Alan Moorehead, **The Russian Revolution**.
4. p. 22, George Lansbury, **My Life**, quoting Keynes at Harvard.
5. p. 308, Webster, **World Revolution, Op. cit**.
6. **Ibid**.

7. p. 309, **Ibid.**
8. p. 41, Cleon Skousen, **Naked Capitalist.**
9. Letter from Rev. B.S. Lombard to Lord Curzin, Mar. 23, 1919, **British White Paper on Bolshevism in Russia.**
10. p. 28, John Stormer, **None Dare Call It Treason,** Liberty Bell Press.
11. Arsene De Goulevitch, **Czarism and the Revolution,** Omni Publications, Hawthorne, Calif.
12. p. 40, Skousen, **Naked Capitalist, Op. Cit.**
13. De Goulevitch, **Czarism and the Revolution, Op. cit.**
14. p. 159, R.H. Bruce Lockhart, **British Agent.**
15. p. 207, **Ibid.**
16. p. 201, **Ibid**
17. Unnumbered insert, **Ibid.**
18. De Goulevitch, **Czarism and the Revolution, Op. cit.**
19. p. 22, Stephen Birmingham, **Our Crowd.**
20. pp. 374-376, Vol. I, House of Representatives Document No. 1868, Gov. Printing Office, 1931.
21. p. 404, B.C. Forbes, **Men Who Are Making America.**
22. p. 37, George S. Viereck, **The Strangest Friendship in History.**
23. pp. 428-430, Birmingham, **Our Crowd, Op. cit.**
24. pp. 225-226, Lockhart, **British Agent, Op. cit.**

CHAPTER 5

1. p. 163, Peter Quennell, **John Ruskin.**
2. p. 128, Satah Gertrude Millins, **Rhodes.**
3. p. 131, Lord Alfred Milner, **The British Commonwealth.**
4. 25th Annual Report Council on Foreign Relations.
5. p. 22, Dan Smoot, **The Invisible Government.**
6. p. A6832, Congressional Record, Sept. 22, 1950.
7. p. 217, Sumner Wells, **Seven Decisions that Shaped History.**

CHAPTER 6

1. pp. 92-94 **U.S. News & World Report,** May 10, 1971.
2. **Redbook Magazine,** August 1961.
3. pp. 73-74, G. Bromley Oxnam, **Personalities in Social Reform.**
4. p. 76, **Ibid.**
5. p. A882, Congressional Record, Feb. 6, 1962.
6. **Philadelphia Inquire,** April 27, 1967.
7. p. 3, Gary Allen, **Who Controls the Press,** American Opinion Reprint
8. p. 55, Karl Marx, **Communist Manifesto,** Gateway Edition.
9. "Czechoslovakians Registered Their Guns," **San Fernando Valley Times,** Vol. 12, No 243, Oct. 12, 1949, A.P. Wire Release.
10. p. 213, Keynes, **Economic Consequences of the Peace, Op. cit.**
11. John Kenneth Gailbraith, **New York Magazine,** September 1970.
12. **Ibid.** Emphasis the author's.
13. James Reston, **New York Times,** May 19, 1971.
14. Col. 3, No. 23, **National Economy and the Banking System,** 76th Congress, 1st session, 1939, Senate Document.
15. **Ibid.**
16. p. 247, Kenan, **The Federal Reserve Bank, Op. cit.**
17. p. 524, **State of the Economy and Policies for Full Employment.** Congressional Report.
18. **U.S. News & World Report,** May 5, 1969.
19. p. 325, Quigley, **Tragedy and Hope, Op. cit.**

Vital & Timely Books
by ROBERT L. PRESTON

BE INFORMED! BECOME AWARE OF WHAT IS <u>VITALLY</u> AFFECTING THE QUALITY OF YOUR AMERICAN LIFE!

ORDER YOURS <u>TODAY!</u>

The PLOT to replace the Constitution

A new constitution has already been written for this nation. This book carefully examines this new constitution, explodes its falacies and exposes its robbery of the rights and freedoms of all Americans. Must reading for those who are concerned about this possible loss of their freedom.

How to Prepare for the Coming CRASH

Learn how to prepare for the coming crash and what you must do to survive the resulting depression. Once prepared, you will be ready for not only the coming depression, but also for power failures, food and services strikes, long term unemployment and illness, floods, earthquakes, tornadoes, hurricanes and war. Get prepared now by reading this tremendous bestseller.

Building your FORTUNE with SILVER

This book reveals the dynamic profit potential of Silver. It explores in depth the dramatic new uses to which Silver is rapidly being applied — and the explosive increase in its consumption. Anyone interested in Silver or those who may have questions about Silver should read this book now!

THE NEWSLETTER
That dares to "tell it like it is!"

YOU HAVE A PROBLEM!
Every day thousands of items and issues create such a panorama of confusion you scarcely know which way to turn. Will inflation get worse? Will there be a depression? Should I rent or buy my home? What should I do with my money? Should I put it in savings or buy stock? Will I lose my job? Will my business improve? Are things really getting worse? Should junior go to college? Somehow you must sort the wheat from the chaff. In these busy times that is a pretty tough job to try all by yourself.

WE HAVE THE ANSWER!
At American Research Institute our trained research personnel clear away the confusion by seperating the important issues from the trivial. Up to the minute information on these key issues is compiled from thousands of sources and placed in our data bank every day. Staff members carefully cross check related items and examine the accumulating information to determine trends, changes and primary and secondary effects.

In the bi-monthly newsletter, *The American Report*, the significant issues affecting the quality of your life recieve the penetrating analysis and tremendous insight of Robert L. Preston, as he personally examines the wealth of material compiled by the research staff of the Institute.

Why face the confusion alone? Let the experts help you! Mr. Preston and the entire staff of the American Research Institute are already providing thousands of people with valuable, up to the minute information through *The American Report*. Those fortunate enough to have received this report have profited tremendously, not to mention the peace of mind and confidence that comes with really knowing what is happening, why, and what to do about it.

The American Report, America's finest newsletter service. Just $28 a year for profit, peace of mind and confidence! SUBSCRIBE TODAY!

HEAR ROBERT L. PRESTON

Now on Cassette Tapes!
• Full Length • Uncut • Recorded Live

Now you can actually hear Robert L. Preston, in the privacy of your own home, as he gives the dynamic and informative lectures which have helped thousands save millions of dollars. These tapes were recorded live, on his extensive lecture tours to appreciative "standing room only" crowds in city after city. Crowds which have paid up to $25 each to hear these very same lectures.

After listening to these fascinating cassettes you will —
UNDERSTAND economics as never before!
COMPREHEND what inflation really is and does!
REALIZE why an economic crash is inevitable!
LEARN how YOU can protect yourself and family!
KNOW how to profit from changing economic controls!

Listeners write — "Most informative thing I have ever listened to," "Learned more about handling money than I did from four years of college economics" — "Once we started listening we couldn't break away" — "Our friends listen in amazement- Mr. Preston is certainly a fascinating and informative speaker."

Listen again and again —
Share the message with friends
Order your cassette tapes today!

ORDER BLANK FOR ROBERT L. PRESTON BOOKS ON BACK OF THIS PAGE.

ORDER FORM

American Report Newsletter $28.00 per year _____

BOOKS — $2.95 Each
(for Quantity price see column A below)

Price X Quantity = Amount

How To Prepare For The Coming Crash—Preston _____ X _____ = _____

Building Your Fortune With Silver—Preston _____ X _____ = _____

How To Be Prepared—Page _____ X _____ = _____

How To Grow Your Own Groceries—Ridley _____ X _____ = _____

BOOKS — $2.00 Each
(for Quantity price see column B below)

Wake-up America—Preston _____ X _____ = _____

The Plot To Replace The Constitution—Preston _____ X _____ = _____

CASSETTE TAPES — $4.95 Each
(for Quantity price see column C below)

How To Prepare For The Coming Crash _____ X _____ = _____

Building Your Fortune With Silver _____ X _____ = _____

The Current Economic Crisis _____ X _____ = _____

SUB TOTAL _____

POSTAGE: USA 20¢ each item
Canada 25¢ each item _____
(orders cannot be shipped without proper postage paid)

TOTAL _____

QUANTITY PRICE

	A	B	C
10 thru 24	2.75	1.80	4.75
25 thru 49	2.65	1.70	4.65
50 thru 99	2.55	1.60	4.55
100 +	2.45	1.50	4.45

Make check payable for the Total and send order to:

JEFFERSON HOUSE
P.O. Box 150
Provo, Utah 84601

Please allow 2 to 4 weeks for delivery.